LAST PLANE
FROM NICE

Also by Clarissa Watson
in Thorndike Large Print

Somebody Killed the Messenger

LAST PLANE FROM NICE

A Persis Willum Mystery

CLARISSA WATSON

Thorndike Press • Thorndike, Maine

Library of Congress Cataloging in Publication Data:

Watson, Clarissa.
   Last plane from Nice : a Persis Willum mystery /
   Clarissa Watson.
   p. cm.
   ISBN 0-89621-963-1 (alk. paper : lg. print)
   1. Large type books. I. Title.
[PS3573.A848L37 1990]   89-77191
813'.54--dc20   CIP

Thorndike Press Large Print edition published in 1990 by
arrangement with Atheneum Publishers.

Cover design by James B. Murry.

This book is printed on acid-free, high opacity paper. ∞

for Nathalie and Roger
who found L'Oasis
and for Robin and Jacques
in whose Paris apartment
this book was written

LAST PLANE
FROM NICE

Chapter 1

The aircraft left the runway with its usual effortless lift and began a graceful arc out over the sea, away from the city, in preparation for the slow turn that would swing it toward its destination north of the Côte d'Azur.

Passengers seated on the right side of the plane could still see Nice and the blue Estérel Massif, the latter ever more faintly, and many leaned close to the small windows, watching. Some watched with indifference, some with nostalgia, the last view of the sun-drenched Elysian coast. Passengers on the left of the aircraft watched the sea below as it began to deepen in color and gradually merged with the horizon somewhere in the direction of North Africa.

People seated in the center seats of the forward section — there was no first class on this flight — having nothing to look at, clamored for the newspapers offered by the hostesses (newspapers were in great demand this summer) and placed orders for soft drinks and champagne served in plastic glasses for twenty-five francs. Tucked in the center of this section was a gaggle of young children returning unaccompanied from camp. They wore large tags, like baggage, and they began an immediate procession to the bathrooms in the front of the aircraft.

The stewardesses, none very young, were moving briskly up and down the carpeted aisles. For them the beginning was classically the hardest part of the flight, the time before everyone settled down, and some of the most experienced had changed on takeoff from the high-heeled black pumps in which they had greeted incoming passengers to more practical flat-heeled footwear.

In the cockpit the captain switched off the seat belt sign. The No Smoking sign was still lit. No one complained; fewer and fewer people were smoking these days. But it wouldn't have mattered if they had. The captain was very senior, with only a year to go before mandatory retirement, and he did much as he pleased; it pleased him not to have his aircraft filled with smoke.

A modest fracas now broke out among the children. One of them, no more than four or five years old, began to wail in a high, piercing voice. There was a minor burst of activity as three stewardesses, all child lovers, rushed to stanch the flow of tears.

During this disturbance a number of passengers on the right aisle suddenly gasped and exclaimed aloud, the sound of their consternation drowned in the child's uproar. One stopped a passing stewardess; she bent over him, looking where he pointed out the window. Then, without a word, she hurried forward to the curtained cockpit section, her silk print dress swinging wildly against sturdy legs. Her smile was bright. Fixed.

Passengers on the right were now murmuring anxiously among themselves, and there was a great forward and backward movement among the aircraft's crew.

The crying child, ignored, had stopped for lack of attention.

A minute or two later the intercom switched on, and the captain's voice, very deep, filled the plane.

"Ladies and gentlemen, this is Commandant Janson speaking. . . ."

Unsteady. Shaken. But only momentarily.

Another try.

"Ladies and gentlemen, I very much regret to tell you . . . something very unfortunate . . . something terrible . . . there has been an explosion . . . the airport . . ."

He did not finish. No one really expected him to.

Chapter 2

It began innocently enough, although the weather was certainly less than innocent, being, in fact, typically Norman.

Sullen black clouds marched in tight ranks across the Channel from Britain, determined to invade the Continent yet one more time. Heavy showers poured down intermittently, dropping spears of rain like sharp-shafted halberds hurled from above by unseen foes crouching in the sky. The wind lashed furiously at anything ill-advised enough to be in its way.

The canny French bourgeoisie, experienced survivors of the local weather, were nowhere to be seen; they were huddled in their houses, waiting for a decent break in the showers.

There were, however, two people mad enough to be outdoors. I was one of them, standing defiantly in the middle of the town square, trying simultaneously to juggle an umbrella, a pencil, and a sketchbook and attempting, not too successfully, to put the finishing touches on a drawing I'd begun the day before. Courseulles-sur-Mer on the Normandy coast has a particularly fascinating World War II monument. All French towns have war monuments of some kind dedicated to the fallen of some war at some time in their history. Courseulles has a small amphibious Sherman tank. What made this tank, named "Bold," so special was that it had been sunk offshore in the D-day landings more than forty years before and lain underwater in the harbor for twenty-seven years until the Canadian units that liberated the town raised the money to refloat it and present it to the village fathers as a memorial. I was making a drawing of "Bold" because everything about the landings interested me; my father had been there. And this little tank, so jaunty and brave, represented to me the essence of the whole incredible undertaking.

So there I was, working away, trying to get it all down on paper, ignoring the filthy weather because it refused to go away and ignoring it was the only way to finish what I'd started.

The other person in the square had just arrived: a small, dark Frenchman oozing out of an even smaller, darker French car and whipping open a giant umbrella that almost engulfed him.

He marched straight toward me.

"Mrs. Willum . . . remember me?"

As I am an artist, I am supposed to have an

13

eagle eye, trained to every nuance, and I more or less generally do. But in a nation of small, dark men no single one is likely to stand out, and I was momentarily baffled. But only momentarily.

"Deauville?" I ventured after a slight hesitation.

"Bravo! Jean Claude Tendron, *à votre service.*"

Jean Claude Tendron, Boy Broadcaster. Of course. Deauville. The opening of the Gainsborough Brown art exhibition that was to end up in Paris next month. My employer, the ubiquitous Gregor Olitsky, had sent me to represent his galleries. Gregor had been Gains's agent when Gains was alive, and he continued to represent the estate now that Gains was dead. But as Gains was definitely dead and wouldn't know the difference and as nothing was for sale and as the really important part would be when the exhibition got to Paris, practical Gregor had elected to save himself for the main extravaganza. He was now off fishing in unknown waters with a client who was not only alive but complete with a yacht that carried a helicopter for spotting hapless marine prey.

Still, yachts and fishing notwithstanding, there was a certain protocol to be observed, and my presence in Deauville had come under that heading. The galleries had to be represented.

There was also the fact that I had painted the one and only (and hence official) portrait of the unfortunate Brown, who had drowned while intoxicated — as usual — in a Long Island swimming pool. I had detested Gains when he was alive, but now, ironically, my portrait of him was shown wherever his work was exhibited and was making me ever so mildly famous — at least famous enough to have been interviewed on Antenne Two of French TV two weeks before.

"Deauville. Yes."

I was remembering perfectly now. He and an equally juvenile crew had interviewed everyone in sight. When my turn came, he'd posed me in front of the Gainsborough Brown portrait and asked a series of idiotic questions. Was Gains a genius? Had I been in love with him? Did I think he painted like Thomas Gainsborough? Did I always carry my sketchbook with me?

I'd done my best to answer everything with a straight face.

Afterward someone whispered to me that Tendron was the son of a famous French anchorwoman and that this was his debut as a broadcaster. That explained a lot.

Now he was looking at me disapprovingly, if a five-foot-two child of nineteen or so could look disapprovingly at a five-foot-four woman

15

of thirty-seven. "I've been searching all over for you. You said you were staying on in Normandy for a while to paint. You specifically mentioned the landing beaches. I remember."

Was I supposed to feel guilty? "My father was at Omaha Beach."

"But where were you? Now, I mean? I tried all the usual places – the Royal, the Normandy, the St.-James, L'Amirauté –"

All the great hotels. I suppose he would. Actually, I had been right here in Courseulles the whole time, trying to stretch a week's expense money into a month's painting tour. My room at the Belle Aurore – harbor view, full pension and terrace included – was about twenty dollars a day. Even so, my funds were evaporating at an alarming rate.

"You've been looking for me? Why?"

He dipped his umbrella at me as if it could seduce me and smiled winningly. "It's one o'clock, and I'm starved. I've just driven all the way from Paris. I'm on my way to London – taking the Hovercraft, helping our anchorman on a story. How about lunch?"

Lunch was a meal I was currently trying to ignore. Guarding the figure, it's called. "I have to finish this."

"Finish it tomorrow. Let's lunch – media artist to painting artist, as it were. Haven't you noticed your paper is soggy and your

16

pencil line is blurring?"

I had. "True. But —"

He wouldn't give up. "Have you by chance also noticed that it's pouring rain?" Waving his black umbrella at the sky.

"Naturally. But it always rains in Normandy."

He couldn't dispute the fact. "Almost always. And that's exactly why I'm proposing Nice."

Just like that he had my full attention. I closed my sketchbook carefully, so the wet pages wouldn't tear, placed it equally carefully in my bag, put my drawing pencil away, and peered at him damply from beneath my own dripping umbrella. What was this? Surely not a real proposition. What then?

"That's right," he continued, beaming. "I propose that you go to Nice. Nice has had thirty-one consecutive days of sunshine — I checked with our weatherman. And it's not unusual. So that's where you go."

Thirty-one days of sunshine had an attractive ring. Better than the song of the Lorelei to someone who had been practically living underwater. "Don't think I haven't dreamed about it."

But it was out of the question. I wasn't going to Nice for the same reason I wasn't staying at the Royal, the Normandy, the St.-James, or the Amirauté: I had a return ticket to America in my purse and little else.

"Impossible."

Tendron's white teeth gleamed through the rain like big Citroën headlights on bright. "I know exactly what you're thinking. You'd love to go, but you can't spare the time to play around on the beautiful Côte d'Azur. You have work to do, you're thinking. Americans always think they have work to do. Am I not right?"

It wasn't the time that I couldn't spare. "Approximately."

"Well, listen to this. Shortly after the Deauville broadcast our station got a call from the Society for the Preservation of Old Nice, a group of well-heeled, public-spirited souls with the time and the money to see to it that the old part of the city doesn't go to ruin. Many French cities have groups like that. Anyway, this society saw the interview and your portrait of Brown, and they've wired plane tickets and a nice retainer and instructions for you to come right down and paint a portrait of the mayor, which they're commissioning as a gift to the city because he's done so much to help their cause. You're to have the use of a villa and a car as long as you're down there."

If he'd dropped the opening bomb of the next world war at my feet, I couldn't have been more astonished. "You're not serious."

"Try me!" With a prestidigitator's flourish he

18

drew a check from some mysterious compartment of his multizippered leather jacket and waved it beneath my nose like bait. "My mother says the people are legitimate, and so is the money. Naturally I checked with her . . . she knows everyone and everything. And listen to this. You're not the only one to profit. The station wants to send me to do an interview when you've finished. The mayor's an important man in France. They're very pleased."

He held the check still for a moment, and I thought I could count five figures. "Don't get it wet, for heaven's sake." Not if there were truly five figures.

"Well, are you interested?"

My mind bounced crazily from point to point. If the check were real . . . if the sunshine were real . . . if the tickets were real . . . if I weren't dreaming . . . Gregor wouldn't mind; he'd get a commission. And there was so much to paint on the Côte d'Azur . . . a working vacation . . . all expenses paid . . .

Tendron was staring at me, had been for some time. His dark eyes were scanning me like a metal detector at an airport. "How tall are you anyway?"

"Tall? About five-four, I guess. Why?"

"How old?"

"Don't be impertinent."

"Sorry. Eyes?"

19

"Would you say gray? I'm not sure. Why?"

He pretended to pat himself on the back. "Congratulations, Tendron – right again. Why? *They* wanted to know. The group. Someone called, asking. To tell the mayor, they said. *He* likes to know."

"How odd."

"Not really. He's very busy, but being a true Frenchman, he would probably drop everything for a good-looking woman. I told them not to worry." He giggled.

Tendron might be a baby, but he knew how to flatter a lady.

He had stuffed the check back in his pocket and zipped the pocket shut. "So, now we will have lunch and discuss the details. We're lunching on Antenne Two, so we can eat like horses. Where can we go in this town?"

I pulled out a handkerchief and mopped at the raindrops that had accumulated on the end of my nose. "The Belle Aurore has a three-fork rating."

The French are very enthusiastic about ratings. They count the number of forks in *Guide Michelin* before they consent to enter a strange restaurant.

And sure enough, Tendron's eyes began to glow with anticipation. "Three forks? We're off!"

The edges of our umbrellas locked like eager

lovers, and we galloped toward his car, splashing water all over our legs. But it didn't matter. We both were feeling great: I felt rich; he felt successful. That's how little it takes when you're two starving "artists."

Somehow he squeezed the two of us and our two umbrellas into his little, dark car, and we rocketed off on two wheels for the Belle Aurore, which was just around the corner. We were going about two hundred extravagant miles an hour.

"En garde, Nice," he shouted, tramping a little harder on the gas. The car switched to one wheel and accelerated to about four hundred miles an hour.

I paled. And then I thought, What the devil? You only live once.

It was going to be glorious. Sunshine. A villa of my own. A car. Mediterranean food and wine. The Riviera. Money in my pocket. And a whole new group of wonderful people.

The people – they would be the best part perhaps. The kind of people I liked – people who dedicated themselves and their money to the art of keeping things beautiful. Idealistic people. Artistic people. Educated people. People helping to preserve the past.

And I would be doing a portrait of a man they admired.

I was going to love it. I'd be crazy if I didn't. "Sunshine, here I come," I cried. "Faster, Tendron . . . faster."

Chapter 3

The Air-Inter plane from Paris, Orly West, to Nice had been filled with expensive-looking passengers, all of them in white despite the fact that it was pouring in Paris — white slacks, white jackets, white Panamas. Even the small dogs some of them carried were white. I understood the reason for the universal color when we stepped out onto the tarmac at our destination: Nice was an inferno.

The climb down the metal staircase from the plane and the short walk across the runway to the terminal left everyone gasping. Inside the building it was worse; the air had an actual physical density. Passengers flailed feebly with their arms to make a passage through it, an effort which exhausted them even further. There was no air conditioning. There were no fans. Only the leaden air and the relentless heat.

Those of us from the Paris flight dragged ourselves slowly through the passage reserved for new arrivals. On either side of the barriers

23

people hung in limp clusters, lackluster eyes searching for those they had come to meet. There wasn't a sound to be heard; the everyday business of breathing was too debilitating for talking. I fumbled in my handbag for the small fold-up Japanese fan I always carry in summer. It helped, but not much.

Someone would be there to meet me. Tendron had promised. Exactly who it would be he hadn't known. But so far none of the bodies draped along the barricade had shown the slightest interest in me. I checked the message board. Nothing. No one at the baggage pickup either.

I had collected my luggage and was wondering what to do when he appeared.

"Mrs. Willum?"

He wasn't at all what I had expected. I disliked him on sight, and I wasn't prepared for that, because I am inclined to like men — all of them.

The first thing I disliked was that he was immaculately cool. Like Jay Gatsby. All in white and perfectly, exquisitely unruffled by the heat or anything else. Whereas I was rapidly dissolving like a melting candle. Everything that makes me worth an occasional second glance — hair, makeup, crisply pressed clothes — was dissolving right before his eyes. Beauty and the Beast. I was the Beast.

"I'm Mrs. Willum." Sulkily.

"Sorry to be late. Traffic."

The second thing I resented was his looks, of course.

It is a well-known fact that I am susceptible to good-looking men, and this one was a beauty. So I should have heard the old familiar drumbeat and the Sousa band pounding out the overture the minute I saw him. Because he was the kind that usually makes me breathe a little faster: tallish, aristocratic, arrogant, and with just the right kind of classy bump on the bridge of his nose.

It was probably his eyes and not some newly cultivated strength of character that saved me. The eyes were wary. And yes — weary. As if nothing he saw could surprise or interest him.

Including me.

He was holding out a photograph for my inspection. "Credentials. By way of identification and introduction."

I saw that it was a picture of Jean Claude Tendron and me standing in front of the Gainsborough Brown portrait at Deauville. For some reason it astonished me. "Where did you get this?"

"We lifted it from the videotape we made of the interview. By the way, I'm Guy Longhi." He didn't bother with a welcoming smile any more than he had bothered with a welcoming handshake.

Longhi. Funny, I thought, a Frenchman with an Italian name. A blondish Frenchman at that. Then I remembered my homework. A hundred and thirty years ago Nice had been called Nizza because it belonged then to Italy. Nice was peopled with Frenchmen of Italian descent.

But why had the society made a tape of the Antenne Two interview? Not that it didn't have a perfect right. Still, it was puzzling. Surely it didn't need a photograph to identify me at the airport; we could have met at the information desk. Or he could have carried a sign with my name on it as the French love to do when meeting strangers. On the other hand, I couldn't imagine him walking around with a sign. And as for the society, maybe it made a tape because it was detail-minded.

He had picked up my bags and was carrying them across the waiting room, leading me with marvelous swiftness through the terminal and outside to a two-seater green Porsche parked under a No Parking sign. The Porsche was new, and shafts of light from the sun shot off its hood and into the air like *feux d'artifice* in the skies over Paris on the fourteenth of July. I couldn't suppress a gasp of admiration; I suppose he heard and chalked it up to peasant origins.

The luggage was quickly stowed, and he motioned me into my seat. The instrument panel, I noted, looked entirely computerized. It probably was. But I didn't ask; this man did not encourage conversation. Instead of talking, I sank back into the soft leather and watched the sights fly by. There were plenty of them.

First the airport, planes parked against a theater backdrop of sea or mountain foothills. Then the long, achingly beautiful stretch of the Promenade des Anglais, with the aquamarine water of the calm Mediterranean on the right and apartment houses of "grand standing" and luxury hotels on the left. A brilliant palette of bathers stretched out in impressionist colors on the rounded white pebbles that substitute for sand. A few small boats bobbing at anchor, a few yachts on the horizon, a giant cruise ship steaming for Corsica, clean-cut and white. Benches painted the exact pale blue of the water lined the sea side of the promenade. Palm trees and flowers, extravagant and exotic. Million-dollar shops flashing by on the left. The majestic Hôtel Negresco, its pink dome gleaming in the sun, its multitude of flags fluttering in the hot breeze coming in from the quiet sea. American flags, Italian, British. And of course, forever and always, the tricolor. In fact, the tricolor was everywhere, flying from everything that would hold it. There were sea blue bleachers set up temporarily along the promenade in anticipation of the next spectacular event: fireworks . . . Batailles de Fleurs . . . parades . . . carnivals.

Nice – my favorite artists had painted it. Everywhere I saw their colors. There was nothing quite like it: jewel shades of sea and sky, its sensual greens, the wild extravagance of its flowers.

We whirled swiftly down the length of the promenade, along the Quai des États-Unis, past the Monument aux Morts below the Chateau, along the edge of the Old Port, where indolent cruisers nuzzled into the minuscule harbor, and began to wind upward. Automobile fumes and motorbikes and vehicles of all kinds accompanied us. Signs appeared, pointing to the three Corniches: the Grande, the Moyenne, and the Inférieure. Other signs to Villefranche and Monaco. A collection of fine five-story orange-and-blue awninged apartment buildings sprang up on either side.

We continued to climb. I saw a sign to Mount Boron, and the Porsche dodged off the main route and followed it. There was little traffic now, although I could still hear it buzzing away behind and below us.

Longhi drove with extraordinary concentration, his neatly defined head turning from side to side, eyes searching both the outside and dashboard mirrors. His indifference to my presence was complete.

Or so I thought.

Then, as I turned toward him, I found myself staring at my own image in the dashboard mirror, which was turned to catch not the reflection of the traffic behind but the reflection of me — Persis Willum. He was using his outside mirror for watching the traffic. And all that concentrated driving and head turning had been so that he could watch the traffic and study me at the same time. No wonder he hadn't spoken; he'd been too busy.

But why?

"I think your mirror needs adjusting, Mr. Longhi."

He reached up and adjusted it, simultaneously whipping us smoothly around a curve with one hand on the wheel. "Happens all the time. Must have it tightened."

Well, maybe.

"This mayor I'm going to paint . . . can you tell me about him?"

"Ribot? Deputy Mayor Jules Ribot — to give him his full title. The whole world can tell you about him; he's made a career of making sure that they can."

"You don't like him?"

"Liking has nothing to do with it. He runs

this place. The society has to work through him or his successor, if he has one, to preserve the Old City, our nearest neighbor, you could say. We flatter. We cajole. We do what we must. We can't let it become a haven for drug addicts and criminals."

"I see."

"As for liking him" – he returned to my remark, apparently stung by it – "one doesn't *like* politicians. They are there to serve. They are the instruments through which we get things done."

"It's a good concept."

He wasn't through. "Americans insist on liking everybody. It's a dangerous fault."

"Actually, I thought our dangerous fault was that we insisted on being *liked*."

He ignored my little jab and returned his attention to his driving. The Porsche shot smoothly up a final steep ascent and halted before the iron gates of a large villa. On the outside wall I saw a polished brass plate. L' OASIS, it said.

"Your new home." He leaned across me to open the door on my side. "My chauffeur is inside. He will bring in your bags."

As I stepped out of the car, I could feel a cool breeze caress my damp cheek and bare arm. Life was going to be bearable after all.

The gate swung open, and I could see masses

30

of flowers and dusty pink blossoms, delicate as tissue paper, drifting across the garden and the walk leading to the house. When I step on them, I thought wildly, I shall feel exactly like a Roman general . . . perhaps one who passed this way . . . having a triumph as he entered Rome. The only thing missing would be slaves in chains accompanying my chariot.

The chauffeur had appeared, young and fit and businesslike. He picked up my bags and waited respectfully for me to step inside the garden.

"When will I begin work?" I asked the cool, indifferent man behind the wheel.

"Don't you read the newspapers?"

On top of everything else, he's not very polite, I thought. "Not when I'm abroad; I read enough bad news when I'm at home."

"Well, perhaps you should. A couple of days before we got in touch with you Ribot was flown out of town secretly to an 'undisclosed destination.'"

"And you still engaged me?"

"We didn't know. Only yesterday his spokesman announced that he is taking a brief 'cure' in Switzerland; it's the classic place."

I detected a deep skepticism in the way he said it. "Do you really think he's ill?"

"Ill? I think not. Ribot's strong as an ox." He

31

exchanged a glance with his chauffeur.

"What then?"

"Who knows? Most probably a car accident
— the French drive like maniacs. Accidents
happen here every minute, especially on the
Corniches. But don't worry, he'll be back soon.
You saw those reviewing stands? There's to be
a big Battle of Flowers in a few days, and he'll
be back for that if they have to prop him up on
sticks and shoot him full of drugs. This town
in summer is like Versailles under Louis the
Fourteenth. The whole world will be here,
including the mayor. You'll see."

The chauffeur motioned me inside the gate.
Longhi bent down and fiddled with something
inside his car. Clearly I was dismissed.

"An accident," I said aloud as I stepped onto
the carpet of drifting pink blossoms.

And I thought I heard Longhi respond from
inside the depths of his Porsche. He said
something, and it sounded like "That failed."

But I must have been mistaken because it was
all so confusing.

A secret flight. Ill health. A possible accident. A chauffeur who waited at the house
while his employer drove the car.

I moved along toward the villa, roses and
climbing geraniums blooming extravagantly on
all sides. A sedate line of palms waved leafy
arms above me. A lemon tree bent low beneath

32

a golden burden. And somewhere a bird cried angrily, "Pea . . . pea . . . pea."

Behind me the gate swung noisily shut. I heard it click and lock.

Chapter 4

L'Oasis had been built on two levels, both of them clinging at different heights to the side of Mount Boron.

The main door, in the French way, opened onto a marble-floored foyer, from which a green-carpeted staircase soared gracefully upward to the main floor. A heavily chased door to the left of the entry opened to a bedroom wing, complete with its own balcony and a glass-walled bath overlooking the sea and the city. The practical necessities of the house — heat, water, etc. — hid tactfully behind a second carved door on the foyer's right.

The whole house must have been freshly painted before my arrival, for the scent of linseed and turpentine was faint but present everywhere.

Upstairs were a library (smelling strongest of paint), a vast drawing room with glass doors opening onto a balcony, a dining room, and a fine kitchen, completely stocked, which had its own balcony for breakfasts.

There were fresh-cut flowers everywhere and great exotic plants rising vigorously from great exotic Chinese pots.

Behind the villa was a garden enclosed in cool, impenetrable vines. All three balconies offered breath-taking views of the pale blue Mediterranean on one side and the foothills of the Alps on the other.

This was a place for an artist — perfect. Here I had everything one could wish for: sunshine, a beautiful place to live and work, and even a breeze.

The whole of that first late afternoon and evening I never moved from my chair on the big front balcony, drowning in the view and the scene that unfolded and shifted and re-grouped itself lazily before me. As I watched, the sky and the blue hills changed slowly to deep purple. Streetlights like drooping jack-o'-lanterns quietly turned to firefly flickers. The sky deepened to black, and a million lights suddenly blazed up. Necklaces of silver and gold wound in soft curves along the coastline. Mysterious flashes danced in the hills as cars traced a magic pattern there. About eleven a golden moon appeared and ever so sedately moved across the sky, towed by unseen hands behind a proscenium stage right.

The breeze, steady, cool, and strong, stayed with me.

I had everything.

Everything, that is, except a sitter and a schedule. But who cares? I thought.

Everything in good time.

When I awoke the next morning, I couldn't understand at first where I was. An angry bird scolded stridently in the palm trees — "pea . . . pea . . . pea." A colony of doves was gossiping in the shelter of the eaves, one of them punctuating the confidences with cries of "I CAN'T go, you fool . . . I CAN'T go, you fool." Most puzzling of all, from a spot I couldn't isolate, someone was whistling the "Marseillaise" in piercing tones — the first line. What could it be: a madman or a bird? *"Allons, enfants de la patrie"* over and over again.

Behind all this uproar the sound of motorcycles floated up from the city as from a factory filled with demented sewing machines at work.

I barely heard the phone when it rang softly and discreetly. French phones today are nonintrusive to a fault.

"I trust you slept well and that you have everything you need? The house was my responsibility because it's my house. I'm Nicole de Plessis, chairman of the board of the society." She sounded warm and welcoming.

"Everything is perfect, thank you. I hope I haven't dispossessed anyone?"

"It wouldn't matter. I have other houses. The one you're in is reserved for special guests. Will you come by for drinks later today? We're very American here in some ways — everyone sees everyone else all the time, and we actually have a cocktail hour. It will give you a chance to look us over. You can't imagine how happy we are to have you; we're thoroughly bored with one another. Seven? And you're invited to dine with us later . . . everything is later here because of the heat."

I was fully awake and oriented now. "I'd love that. Where are you?"

"Directly behind you up on Mount Boron. In fact, I can look down on you. We all can. We're scattered all around up here."

If there were villas on Mount Boron behind L'Oasis — and there obviously were — they were well hidden. The scenery in that direction looked pure and unspoiled, blanketed with black trees and an occasional palm under a cloudless sky.

Below L'Oasis the scene was entirely different. Orange-roofed bourgeois houses tumbled modestly downhill until they came to a stop against the newer apartment houses that in turn tumbled down into the crowded streets that bordered the Old City. All this was merely the bottom of the frame that enhanced the magnificent view, the only discordant note of which was a single five-story apartment house that had somehow managed to get itself built on the rapidly descending ground to the right of my front balcony, its own wraparound balcony on a level with mine. I had the impression that this was a fairly decent building and the man I had seen on the balcony late the night before — thin, bare-chested, and bronzed — had also looked fairly decent in his crisp white shorts.

De Plessis was still talking. ". . . gates on left . . . sign says TOUJOURS GAIE . . . living up to the name . . . remember, seven."

"Seven," I repeated. Toujours Gaie?

It was going to be interesting.

Chapter 5

I saw at once that she was one of those women who are impervious to age, probably one who, when the law of gravity makes it necessary, rushes off to the great Ivo Pitanguy or an equally gifted doctor for help. There are many magicians in the world who know how to perform miracles that arrest women in a Shangri-la of ageless beauty, but Pitanguy is special: He changes his mountains of gold into free operations for the poor, to repair the disfigured, the burned, the hopeless. This makes the rich ladies happy; they go under the knife knowing that their vanity is supporting a noble cause.

Whatever her age, Nicole de Plessis was unquestionably a distinguished and arresting woman. Her skin was so transparent and white that one could identify every vein that carried the patrician blue blood circulating beneath it. Her perfect black hair was drawn back from a perfect oval face. A perfect diamond, so large that it barely escaped being vulgar, gleamed on a perfect slender finger.

She crossed the room in one flowing motion to greet me, yards of filmy beige gown floating lightly around her.

"Persis Willum, of course . . . I recognize you from the tape."

The room had been done to match her, or she to match the room; everything was in beige and white with a few careful black accents to enhance the effect. There was a single concession to color: shafts of red and yellow bursting from a large Bonnard on the far wall.

I had timed my arrival for the obligatory ten minutes late, but the room was already crowded. The French can be disconcertingly prompt. When I entered, they all stopped and looked at me.

"I'm Nicole de Plessis. They've all been waiting to see you. Let me introduce you. If some of them look like cutthroats, don't worry. Their ancestors may have been, but this lot has reformed."

She drew me to a seated ancient person covered almost entirely in dark blue taffeta. Little could be seen of her except a small balding head topped by a knot of stringy hair anchored to her pate by a jeweled comb.

"Princess Anna, may I present Mrs. Willum? You'll have to shout at her, I'm afraid; she's quite deaf. And don't be frightened when she speaks to you, her voice is very loud. Luckily

40

she doesn't speak often."

A knotty, transparent, blue-veined hand darted out suddenly from the mounds of taffeta and presented itself. I wondered if I was supposed to kiss the imperial claw; and while I was debating, it withdrew itself and disappeared again.

"She lives in a marvelous villa — what we call here a *folie* — built in the period when Nice first received distinguished European visitors with the arrival of the railway in 1864. Two imperial locomotives appeared then, crowded with princes, bankers, and adventurers following in the wake of Queen Victoria and the Czarina Alexandra Feodorovna, and everyone started to build delicious, delirious, exotic madnesses. You'll see!"

A middle-aged, rather seedy-looking type had detached himself from the crowd and was bearing down on us.

"Here's Mario," my hostess said. "Mario Guarnieri — you're probably too young to remember his name. He was a famous Grand Prix driver — the best of his era. And he still likes to do everything fast."

He was bowing over my hand. There was a perfect round bald spot on the top of his head, not unlike the princess's. "Not so fast anymore, Nicole. I'm in low gear these days." He straightened up, and I saw that his eyes were like two

41

rather nice, soft crèmes caramels. I liked him instantly.

"Mario is an intellectual illiterate but a physical marvel who has married several rich widows and now is also rich."

He didn't resent it. "I loved them all," he said, and smiled. His nose, I saw, had been broken many times and never properly set; it wandered vaguely around on his face like a tourist wandering around the Louvre searching for the *Mona Lisa.* He was dark from the sun — all the men here were — and he was wearing green linen slacks with sea gulls embroidered on them, which could have come from the Gull Harbor Club on Long Island or Lyford Key, Bahamas.

A new face had appeared, this one round as a plate with barely any features to mar its flatness. "Jim Gallop Mustard," it said. "I wrote *Love Lives of the Superrich.*"

It must have been at least fifteen years ago. "I've heard of it."

"Everybody has. It's his claim to fame," de Plessis said.

A terrible noise, somewhat like boulders crashing down a mountain, filled the room. "Dey vas orderink hit mans." After an instant's astonishment I realized that the princess had spoken. By the time I worked that out she had again retreated into her lizardlike immobility.

"It's true," Mustard told me happily. "Those women actually put out contracts on me. I had to buy them off and retreat here, to the Continent."

I didn't believe him for a moment; but it was a good story, and the girl leaning against the piano was obviously aware of it. "He's been dining out on that tale ever since he came to live here," she said, smiling. "Mustard's completely outrageous."

This girl seemed familiar to me. I was sure I'd met her before, but I couldn't think where or when. She was quite a beauty, in a different sort of way: tall, pencil-thin, small of feature, with a face framed in a glow of red-gold hair. Where had I known her? I couldn't think.

Then Mustard explained. "She's Julie Savage. Her mother is Victoria Savage."

"Of course." I should have known; I'd seen enough photographs of the mother. I ought to have recognized the daughter immediately. Victoria Savage. Who of any age hadn't seen her films in revival or on late-night TV? Who didn't remember the story of her doomed alliance and how her health and her career were destroyed when it was learned that underworld money had backed her last European film? Julie was the issue of all that — a disgrace at the time.

Gregor had known Victoria Savage. He still

43

grew misty-eyed when he recalled her. "The most beautiful and vulnerable woman in the world," he'd said. "I understand that she lives in a villa somewhere in the south of France with nurses 'round the clock. No expense spared for her comfort since her breakdown. Her daughter takes care of everything."

Now I knew where that villa was — here, in the hills behind me.

"Julie's a beauty, isn't she?" The newcomer was a perfect prototype of a French girl: small, slender, a fringe of black bangs, and an insolent slash of red lips. I started to answer in French, but she interrupted.

"Don't let the looks fool you. I'm from Buffalo. Mrs. James Gallop Mustard, for what it's worth, which isn't much these days. B. B. Benezit, if you happen to read art critics."

So that's who she was — the notorious B. B. Benezit, who admitted she'd picked her name from the cover of the most famous art dictionary in the world. She'd then gone on not only to write blistering critiques of all the sacred cows in the art world but to produce a famous film about an artist who "painted" his pictures by rolling nude models first in paint and then across a blank canvas. She'd been a big name once. But like her husband's best seller, that had also been long ago. Neither of them had been heard from lately.

"I'm so pleased to meet you." I was.

Mario interrupted. He did not intend to let me linger. "You must see Nicole's view. It's the best on the Côte d'Azur. Come." And he led me outdoors, to a terrace that ran the length of the villa.

He was right; the view was incomparable. The first thing I noticed was a superb view of my villa, just as Nicole had said. After that there was an even more superb view of the coastline, just as Mario had promised. Up here the breeze was even cooler than at L'Oasis.

"You'll end up like the rest of us after you've been here awhile: You'll never want to leave."

I could believe it. "When do you think I'll start work?"

"Any minute. A day or so at most."

"That's not true. He's lying to you."

The newcomer was as dazzling as the view itself. He gleamed with gold chains and bracelets and watches and Gucci and hand-painted silk. He had assumed a graceful pose, one leg forward, as if photographers were expected. He was quite beautiful, in fact.

"Robin Wilson." Guarnieri sighed, sounding resigned. "Robin, so this is where you've got to. Mustard's been looking all over for you."

"Let him look!"

"Are you sulking?" Mario turned to me to explain. "Nicole kicked him out of L'Oasis to make room for you. Originally Mustard found him downtown on his uppers. The rock band he was with had foundered. That was several years ago."

The elegant young man's voice rose an alarming octave. "Not true!"

"He's been Nicole's favored house pet ever since."

"Not true — none of it. I wasn't with a rock band. I'm a dancer, between engagements. And I'm not Nicole's pet — you know it perfectly well. And why don't you tell her the truth about Ribot?"

"What truth?" Guarnieri looked more amused than annoyed by all this temperament.

"Ribot's people may have the French press fooled, but not the British and not me. I managed to get my hands on this before all the copies were bought up or withdrawn."

He had been holding a folded newspaper tight against his elegant thigh. Now he whipped it up and open. It happened very fast — a split second. But I saw the newspaper. And I saw what it said before Guarnieri snatched it away and strode out of the room.

Only a split second. But it was enough.

It was the *Daily Mail.*

And the headline shrieked:

46

EXCLUSIVE!
ASSASSINATION ATTEMPT ON MAYOR OF NICE!

and underneath that:

FUTURE PRESIDENTIAL CANDIDATE WOUNDED!

Robin Wilson was uttering cries of outrage in a furious soprano. "My newspaper . . . how dare you . . . come back . ."

After a moment's surprise I started into the house after Guarnieri. But he had lost himself in the crowd that now filled Toujours Gaie. It appeared that Nicole had invited not just the board but *all* the members of the society to today's festivities and that every one of them was determined to waylay Persis Willum. The members-at-large clutched at me, embraced me, and congratulated me unrestrainedly on my as-yet-to-be painted portrait of their noble mayor.

I was engulfed in the din of many languages spoken in many accents and all rolling together into one continuous roar that sounded like an approaching metro train. I could scarcely breathe, let alone hear. Most of these people were expatriates and determined to let me know they were delighted to meet a new face.

I suppose I looked desperate because Nicole

47

de Plessis materialized suddenly and rescued me.

"You must come into the other room, Persis . . . people there are dying to meet you."

"They're not the only ones who are dying . . . this is an unbelievable crush. I'm not used to all this attention. Have you seen Mario?"

We were back in the drawing room. Someone was playing the piano. It sounded good.

"He has a newspaper. It says something about an assassination attempt on the mayor."

"Oh, that." She laughed. At least it looked as if she laughed; I couldn't actually hear with all the noise. "Robin already showed me that rag. Mario didn't want you to see it and worry. Don't believe a word of it. The British press never gets a story straight – anything for a headline. Ribot's just off taking the waters or something . . . maybe a tryst, who knows? But you may be sure he's too smart to get himself shot." She was maneuvering me across the room like a general funneling troops through a pass. "I want you to meet the other members of the board. First, Chauncy and Elizabeth Clough-White. She works for us as secretary and treasurer . . . those jobs nobody wants . . . and all without pay, in spite of the fact that they're dirt poor. They have a little servant's cottage up here, you see, and they're as anxious to preserve our way of life as the rest of us."

The Clough-Whites didn't look dirt poor to me, just British. She was decked out in an anonymous print frock with an uneven hem, and he sported the khaki shorts and knee-length socks of a Bermuda escapee. Clough-White acknowledged my presence and launched immediately into a tirade about crime in Libya and Syria and Iran and France and Italy — a tirade I had evidently interrupted.

A fanatic, I thought, smiling attentively and not really listening, a bore and a fanatic on law and order. Oh, dear.

"You have a burglar alarm in your villa?"

I looked at Nicole. "It's broken," she said. "They're all always broken."

"Well, you must have it fixed. Immediately."

"Nonsense," Nicole told him. "Nobody needs them here."

"Yes," I murmured. "I had the impression that Jules Ribot kept crime out of Nice. I had the impression it was why I was doing this portrait."

Clough-White leaped to the mayor's defense. "That's true. He has performed miracles. There are special police in the Vieille Ville with magnum revolvers and Spanish-type AS-TRA caliber three fifty-seven weapons . . . they're called the mayor's cowboys — *les cowboys du maire*. The municipal police are considered first-rate, the best in France, Ribot claims.

There are a hundred twenty of them with three vans, five heavy cars, fifty motorcycles, fifty cycles, and fifty portable radios. Then we have the state police and the airport police and the Brigade des Moeurs. This doesn't count the fire department and the thirty-seven-hundred volunteer force for civil protection which can be mobilized in less than two hours —"

"Enough, enough," Nicole cried. "We all know what he's done . . . that's why we're honoring him."

I was impressed. "You certainly have a gift for remembering statistics."

His wife's plain face, unsullied by any trace of make-up, arranged itself in a stiff smile. "Clough-White has such perfect recall of facts and faces that the army used him as a computer during World War Two, before computers were invented."

"How interesting." I smiled. They smiled.

"Until dinner," they said politely, turning away.

"We pay for their dinners," Nicole explained as they retreated. "It's in lieu of salary. Clough-White has the appetite of the original Neanderthal man and wouldn't miss a paid-for meal for anything. Also, it's a chance for him to deliver his crime lectures to a captive audience — us. Very tiresome." Then she laughed. "But things could be worse. In fact, they are. I'm about to present you to the richest and most loathsome man on Mount Boron, Anton Franck. He *pours* money into our cause, hoping to be made a member of our board, so far without success."

The richest and most loathsome man on Mount Boron was chatting with the best-looking and least friendly man on Mount Boron – Guy Longhi. At our approach Longhi drifted off into the crowd.

"Anton, this is our charming artist."

He was short and thick, as if a heavy weight had been placed on top of him at birth to compress him. He looked like a neglected lawn. Tufts of hair sprouted from him everywhere. Everywhere, that is, except his head, which was totally bald.

"I was the one that picked you out," he announced, making no effort to disguise the fact that he was looking me over, eyes lingering pointedly on vital spots.

"You . . . ?"

"That's right – picked you out. I knew Ribot would go for you. He's a beauty lover."

"He's an *art* lover," Nicole corrected. "Knows all about it – unlike me. I just like things to be pretty."

Franck's eyes hadn't stopped for a minute their inventory of my body. I understood for the first time what people meant when they said something made their flesh crawl.

"He's been shot. I just saw the headline in the *Daily Mail.*" If I expected a reaction from him, I didn't get it. He didn't even blink.

"Nonsense," Nicole said. It seemed to be one of her favorite words. "He's just off having a love affair somewhere. No one could shoot him; his security's too good."

Franck, equally unperturbed, offered another scenario.

"Probably having plastic surgery; all the candidates do it."

"But I saw —"

They laughed.

"Nobody pays attention to the British press. It's the *French* press he has to watch out for. . . ."

"Believe me," Franck said, "you mustn't worry. I've already seen that paper. Guarnieri just showed it to me. Everybody's having a good laugh. The only press more inflammatory than the British is the American — excuse me — I didn't mean to offend you."

He hadn't. "It's all right."

"The French press is swarming all over the place now that he's a potential candidate. How did he deal with the Mafia? What does he like or dislike? How's his love life?"

They played a duet with each other, their speculations making a counterpoint pattern that was hard to separate.

". . . taking a 'cure.' "

". . . remember Giscard's sealed envelopes?"

". . . getting 'done over' . . . typical politician's ego . . ."

". . . probably to look good for his portrait . . . and for the big Gainsborough Brown exhibition in Paris."

Suddenly there was silence, the kind that is always described as thunderous. The kind that always follows a class A faux pas. Franck's face had turned the color of freshly made brick.

"I'm so sorry," Nicole said.

He didn't answer, just turned away and pushed into the crowd, his squat body jostling other bodies to left and right.

"Oh, damn," she said, staring after him. "Our biggest donor — and I've trod on his pride."

"How?" I was mystified.

"The big festivities for the opening of the Gainsborough Brown show in Paris. The president of the republic is host. It's to be one of the affairs of the year. We've all received our invitations."

"So?" I was still mystified.

"So he didn't. He and Robin Wilson. We're board, you see. They're not."

It was still incomprehensible. "Does it matter?" It certainly didn't matter to me. I hadn't received an invitation, and I couldn't care less. It was Gregor's turn; he wouldn't want me there to steal even one ounce of his thunder, and that was all right with me. It was just an art exhibition after all.

"It definitely does . . . to Franck. Those invitations are a sign of having arrived socially. And if there's one thing he wants, it's social respectability."

I linked my arm in hers. "Look at the bright side," I told her. "It proves one thing, at least: Money can't buy everything."

"He's finding that out," she said, laughing.

And arm in arm, like comrades who had just survived a dangerous skirmish undaunted, we plunged back into the fray.

Chapter 6

I could see that dinner was going to be an event of some kind. "Eating is our local pastime," Nicole had said, and it was immediately apparent that she spoke the truth.

The name of the restaurant was La Barracuda, and it was so crowded by the time we arrived that the only way our party of twelve managed to squeeze itself into seats along the mirrored wall was by ceasing entirely to breathe. Once we were safely seated, the food immediately established that we were participants in an important event — one wreathed in flames, like Rome burning.

On Nicole's advice, we all chose the same main course, loup au Fenouil — fish flamed in that favorite liqueur of the Côte d'Azur, pastis. Twelve loups simultaneously afire would warm the heart of the most avid pyromaniac. Dessert was equally fiery. After almost religious consultation we all voted for crepes in creme de cacao and sugar, with orange and lemon squeezed over them at table by our *patron* himself and set ablaze in great cascades of Grand Marnier. All this was accompanied by gallons of Côtes de Provence. "Very good, you know . . . it's local," they explained.

With all the flames and excitement there was little opportunity for conversation, let alone questions, although I had a number of them I was longing to ask. The only thing I managed was a quick question to Nicole about my neighbor across the way.

"Who is the man who has the balcony across from me?"

"You mean in that apartment building? I swear they built it overnight while we all were sleeping. I did the only thing possible: I bought it. The man? Oh, nobody – just a fellow who's renting one of my flats."

"And L'Oasis . . . I hope you didn't have it painted just for me."

But they were already getting up and wandering off in twos and threes for an after-dinner stroll in the nearby gardens of Albert the First, named after Queen Victoria's husband. Tonight the gardens were filled with people of all ages, accompanied by infants and dogs, seated on folding blue metal chairs and listening to a small band playing its heart out in a covered Victorian bandstand. Those who weren't seated were dancing: ample countrywomen jigging modestly together; small children standing on their grandfathers' shuffling feet; big children dragging little children around the floor. It looked like a version of Renoir's *Moulin de la Galette;* the participants in the scene had the same pink-cheeked, black-eyed beauty, the same rounded simplicity.

"Come along, Persis, we're off to the pedestrian mall to take a coffee."

"I'll be right along." But I didn't move; I was enchanted.

"The best shops . . . Jourdan, Chanel, La Roche, Vuitton —"

I wasn't seduced. "Don't wait. I'll be along."

"Well, do hurry. And don't get lost. Look for the lights." They were gone. Smiling. Elegant. Quickly bored.

Now everyone who could was dancing. One tiny laughing boy in a miniature version of a track suit was being swung around by the neck by an older laughing girl. A middle-aged woman in a U.S.A. T-shirt was dancing with a teen-age youth. One girl was dancing entirely alone, lost in a private dream. I wanted to stay longer, to stay until it ended. But I didn't dare, so I headed for a blaze of lights and a series of large fountains. They had mentioned shops. I saw a street lined with arcades and shops before me.

There were lighted windows and people drinking wine. I saw the Galeries Lafayette.

What was it they had said — a pedestrian mall? But there was traffic here.

I looked up, searching for a street sign, not always the easiest thing to find in a French city. But there it was: RUE DE LA LIBERTÉ, it said. And that was not all. Engraved on the same wall were these words:

ANGE GRASSO
FRANC TIREU
PARTISANS FRANÇAIS
FFI
EUT PENDU ICI
LE 7 JUILLET 1944
ET RESTA EXPOSÉ
POUR AVOIR RÉSISTE
Á L'OPPRESSEUR
HITLERIEN

passant
incline toi
souviens toi

Two partisan fighters — hanged on this spot and left exposed for having resisted Hitler's oppression. Bow your head in passing. Remember.

I stopped. I bowed my head. I closed my eyes. I will remember you, whoever you were, I

58

thought. I will honor you.

Everything swirled on around me: the lights, the people, the traffic sounds. I didn't notice. More than forty years ago. A truck driving up. Townspeople assembled on command. Soldiers. Guns. Two young men, arms bound. A command. The truck driven out from beneath them.

"You're drawing attention, Maria, *move on*." The words were whispered. "Are you crazy, standing here?"

I opened my eyes. "Sorry?"

I barely had a glimpse of him because he melted into the crowd the moment I looked around.

Crazy? Maria – do I look like a Maria?

And then I thought, Maybe I misunderstood. Or maybe I didn't. But what did that prove? So I looked like somebody named Maria, and when he saw I wasn't, he decamped. I wouldn't be the first person to be mistaken for somebody else. No one in this world is unique.

I retraced my steps and turned into the pedestrian mall. They were seated at one of the many restaurants that spilled onto the street, sipping coffee and watching the performing magicians and clowns and the milling crowds. They had saved a seat for me.

"Coffee, Persis?"

"Yes, please."

"We were beginning to worry about you."

"No need."

"We thought you might get lost."

"Oh, no."

"Then let's have a cognac to celebrate your being here." B.B. Benezit's black eyes were sparkling with mischief. "I hope at least you had a small adventure?"

Had I? I doubted it. If I had, it was a very small adventure.

"I don't think so," I told them.

"Good," said Longhi. "Better to save yourself for the adventure of reading all about Ribot in the material we're sending over to you tomorrow. That will be adventure enough."

And they all laughed and drank their cognac.

I laughed with them. But I wondered, Had I perhaps had an adventure after all?

"Are you crazy, standing here?"

No. I was right the first time. It hadn't been a very big adventure. I hadn't even seen what he looked like.

Chapter 7

Morning dawned sunny and reasonably cool.

I set off early on foot to market at the top of my street. Everything was there: the *poste*, the butcher shop, the drugstore, the supermarket, and the *boulangerie*, which had the longest line. The next longest line was at the newspaper store. Those days all France was wrapped up in its favorite national pastime – politics. Every day newsstands were stormed for the latest editions of the latest news by citizens hoping for a juicy scandal of some kind.

Because I was more interested in news of Jules Ribot (of which there seemed to be a dearth) than in news of other presidential hopefuls, I hadn't bothered to buy *Nice Matin;* the headlines made it instantly clear that there was no news of *him*.

I had toiled up the hill and was now toiling down again, bowed under the weight of my fresh fruit and vegetables and my bottles of Évian and Côtes de Provence – afoot because there was practically no place to park at the market and almost everyone marketed on foot and early, to beat the heat.

As I paused to shift the weight of my burdens and incidentally to profit from the moment to admire the view of Nice — a view that never ceased to beguile me — I heard a motorcycle careening down the hill behind me. Motorcycles always careen in France; it has, I believe, something to do with the French image of virility. And this one was no exception. It came down the hill as if it had been fired out of a flawed cannon on an uncertain trajectory. And then, when it was almost upon me, so close that there was no question of who the person bowed down by the day's purchases could be, it slammed on its brakes and attempted to slow its headlong descent, for all the world as if it had lost me in the marketplace and was relieved to have found me again.

It skidded, sending a shower of pebbles rattling against my bare leg. It stung.

"Watch it, you idiot!" I shouted angrily.

The motorcycle nearly toppled over. And then it did topple over, sending the rider skidding across the road.

Of course, I was instantly sorry for calling names. I set down my burdens on the sidewalk — remembering to be gentle because of the wine — and rushed out into the street to lend a hand.

The rider was already struggling to his feet and righting his cycle.

"Are you all right? Can I help?"

Now that I was close to him, I was doubly sorry to have shouted. Because I had the impression that he was someone I knew or had seen before.

"You all right?" I asked again.

There was no reply, although I knew he heard me.

The motorcycle righted itself and went its way, at no less heedless a pace, and I thought for perhaps the millionth time that the French and their vehicles have a kind of love affair with death.

And I also thought, That was someone I know.

Longhi's chauffeur? The man on the rue de la Liberté? The man on the balcony across from my villa?

Even with the helmet he was wearing — the helmet that makes everyone look like men from Mars — I was sure of it.

But who?

Chapter 8

My work of the day was to begin reading the mountains of material Longhi's chauffeur had delivered at the crack of dawn. The pile of clippings and photocopies and magazines and documents was intimidating. It would probably take several days to digest and interpret it all.

But I was grateful to have it. I wanted to get to know my man. So I rolled down the orange-and-white-striped awning over my front balcony, settled into a comfortable chair, and went to work.

The morning flew by. Then the afternoon. I didn't notice; I was too fascinated. It was like reading a novel.

Ribot had been born in 1925, son of the owner of a small café in the Old Port who had miraculously managed to accumulate enough funds to educate his son at the Lycée Masséna, where he was remembered as being number one in the *parties de foot* disputed in the court of the *bahute*, whatever that meant. His fellow students later described him as very big and very strong – *"trés gros et trés fort."*

There was more than a drop of Corsican blood in him. His mother and her family had come from Aspretto, where the French train their combat swimmers. His Corsican blood, his admirers said, made him *trés* Napoleon, *trés* Bonaparte. And looking at the many photographs of him, I could see what they meant. He had heavily carved lips, suggesting great power and sensuality, and a slightly thickened nose. Unlike Bonaparte, however, he seemed to be quite tall and powerfully built, with the still intact dynamism of a recently retired athlete. He kept a villa in Corsica, and he also kept a yacht at Beaulieu.

By 1942, at seventeen, he had become a member of the Resistance and a hero. After the war, he was awarded a *brevet de Gaullisme* for his service. Later he prepared his CAPA (*certificat d'aptitude à la profession d'avocat)* at Nice and began to practice law. After a few years of successful practice he turned to politics, eventually succeeding the popular former mayor, upon his retirement, on a platform of continuing the latter's war on organized crime, which had successfully infiltrated the casinos of the Côte d'Azur and taken over the rule of all the gaming places.

His pledge to KEEP THE MAFIA OUT – KEEP NICE CLEAN FOR TOURISM had been the keystone of his success; tourism was the chief source of income for the queen city of the Azure Coast. But Ribot hadn't rested there. Having kicked the Mafia out of Nice, he had undertaken a vigorous campaign to lure international, non-polluting high-tech industries as a backup for tourist income. "We cannot be a one-income city" was his constant cry. And his success had been electrifying: Industry was flocking to Nice.

The mayor was not married. The mayor had never been married. But evidence of his masculinity was plentiful. There were countless photographs of him surrounded by beautiful women; they were omnipresent as he greeted heads of state, welcomed rock stars, opened benefits, met with royalty, dedicated sports stadiums, presented trophies, cut ribbons, was interviewed on TV.

They all looked like Paris models, these women. Maybe they were. "I am a worshiper of beauty," he often said. Apparently.

Anyway, it was obvious that he didn't lack for glamorous companions. If he chose to remain a bachelor, it had to be because he preferred it that way.

Other things were also obvious. He was still, for example, extremely fit. There were dozens of pictures of him playing tennis, surfing, emerging from the waters of the Baie des

Anges, joining in a game of soccer, taking a turn with a visiting rugby team.

And there were less obvious but equally certain conclusions to be drawn. He had a genius for promotion. He had charm.

And he had to be street-wise and smart to have risen so meteorically from such humble beginnings. Had to be, although there was no proof in what I read.

There were other things.

Ribot was an artist *manqué*. "It is my one frustration," he was quoted as saying, "that I have no talent. The desire, the appreciation, but not the talent." He had discovered this sad fact, he said, after hundreds of dollars spent on unsuccessful art lessons.

"I have the eye but not the hand."

So he had turned "appreciator."

"I collect beautiful things. Women. Objects. Paintings."

He had acquired, in fact, some little renown as a collector, concentrating — not surprisingly — on painters of the Riviera.

"The living ones," he said in an interview. "I can't afford the dead ones. I'm just a humble public servant."

Humble or not, his interest in the arts wasn't doing him any harm with the voting public. The French like their politicians cultured. *Culture* is not a dirty word in France.

"Men . . . women . . . paintings . . . they're all a part of art — just as the Riviera itself is — just as France herself is."

A smart man. A good athlete. A consummate politician.

By the end of the day I had learned a lot about Ribot. I knew all the public, superficial facts about him. Now I would have to reread and digest the mountain of material, sort it all out. The portrait artist must paint not only what he sees but what he *knows* if he wishes to produce a painting he is proud of.

I would have to try to understand what the man with the sensual mouth and the bright, professional smile was like beneath his smooth and glittering surface.

What had the board members said to me last night, referring to my learning all about Ribot? "That will be adventure enough."

It wouldn't surprise me if they were right. I suspected that they usually were. And I put the *Daily Mail* headline out of my mind.

Hadn't they all said it wasn't true?

Chapter 9

The next two days saw my life fall into a routine that was to become a pattern, a routine of work and play in a half-and-half recipe that I found delicious.

In the mornings I drove myself down to the beach and stretched out in my very proper one-piece bathing suit to work on my clippings, my sketchbook, and my tan. I did a lot of thinking, too, trying to imagine how I would paint the mysterious missing mayor, and when I would finally get to meet him, and what, if anything, was keeping him out of sight. It was an intriguing puzzle.

Then I lunched with one, several, or all members of the board, sometimes on the beach, sometimes elsewhere.

The odd thing about the beach was that I hadn't thought at first I would like it. Gull Harbor, where I live, has beaches of perfect golden sand; here there were only round white stones called *cailloux*, which hurt the soles of my feet and made me hop like a grasshopper on live coals. They also rolled and clanked in the wash, causing my entries and exits from the Mediterranean to consist largely of slippings and fallings and unprintable remarks.

It was Nicole who saved me. "You really must stop going in and out of the water like an agonized crab, Persis." And she showed me where to buy the plastic sandals everyone wore, even in the water, and where to rent a cot (ten francs), a beach umbrella (also ten francs), a floating mattress (twelve francs), and anything else one wanted.

The Nice beach is dotted with restaurants, and when the board members joined me there for lunch, which was often, the conversation was casual; in fact, as Gregor Olitsky would say, it was rather "ditsy." They speculated about the mayor. They gossiped about each other. They discussed upcoming social events and whether or not they were worth attending. They bantered and jousted, idly and endlessly.

"Where is Ribot?"

"Will he be back for the Bataille de Fleurs?"

"What a pity Julie is saddled with Victoria."

"But she loves it. It's her way of making it up to her mother for everything that happened."

"Has anyone seen her — Victoria, I mean?"

"Not for years. The last few times I called I was always told she was resting."

"Poor Nicole, what a history of love affairs,

no? The biggest one didn't turn out so well, after all. And Robin . . ."

"When do you suppose Ribot will resurface?"

"Nicole. Such a clever woman. But I'd say an unfortunate judge of men, wouldn't you?"

And that's how it went. Sun. Waves. Food. Gossip. The *pirates de la plage* softly calling their illegal wares as they patrolled the forbidden beach — "Pizza . . . Co-ca-Colaa . . . glace . . . pan bagnat." Naked babies. Men in rubber bathing caps stepping gingerly into the sea and swimming back and forth with dignified breast-strokes. Topless girls flirting with everyone in sight. Water parachutists filling the air and *planches à voile* filling the water. The *sapeurs-pompiers* sailing by on patrol, eight to a boat, sitting rigidly upright as if on parade.

The afternoons also assumed a routine. While the board was napping off its Lucullan lunches or tending to board affairs, I sallied forth into the countryside, sketchbook in hand, to fulfill my promise to myself to record the landing sites of the 1944 liberation.

But not everyone slept, as I discovered on the second day.

I had chosen to go to Le Lavandou because it was the site of a landing seventy days after Normandy. There hadn't been enough landing craft for two simultaneous debarkments, so the south of France had had to wait until boats

71

were freed up from Normandy.

I was wandering through the countryside with my sketchbook when I saw a familiar figure – Mario Guarnieri – deep in conversation with one of the local farmers. Farms and fields didn't seem to me to be Guarnieri's style, but there he was, unlikely though it seemed.

"Mario . . . what are you doing here?"

I've seen a few startled men in my life, but Mario was something else. He recoiled like someone shot with a crossbow. Then he spoke to his companion, and the latter hustled off.

"I'm on a painting expedition," I went on. "The Allies landed here."

"Oh?" I had the impression that he was more interested in the fast retreating form of the old farmer he had been talking to than in me.

"But this is scarcely your turf. What are you up to?"

"Up to?" He seemed to take offense, in a flustered sort of way. "Didn't you know I collect World War Two vehicles . . . Jeeps, command cars, tanks? I own about fifty of those artifacts, all in working order."

Of course. Driving was his profession. "You expect to find relics still rusting away up here?"

He began to talk, a man hoping either to gain time or to gather his wits – maybe both. "The first unit to land in the middle of the night of August fourteenth, 1944, in Provence was a

72

unit of French commandos from Africa. They called the whole thing Operation Dragon. It involved two hundred thousand ships, including survivors of the French fleet which sank itself twelve months earlier to escape dishonor: the *Montcalm,* the *Georges-Leygues,* the *Emile Bertin,* the *Dugay-Trouin,* the *Terrible,* the *Fantasque,* the *Malin,* the *Gloire.*" He rattled off the names like a clever schoolboy hoping to distract his teacher from some recently perpetrated mischief.

"I read about it. French sailors mistakenly machine-gunned by British Spitfires, ten thousand men and their parachutes blanketing the valleys of Argens and Nartuby. But there can't be anything left now — that was decades ago."

He still looked flustered, not his style at all. Then he appeared to come to a hasty decision. "I'm working on an important paper to present this August at the anniversary . . . a paper on the landings as remembered by the survivors."

"I see. How old were you when it happened?"

"Just twelve."

"Were you in Nice at the time?"

"Yes."

"Those boys who were hanged . . . Grasso and Tireu . . . I think those were their names . . . were you —"

"There were episodes like that every day back

73

then." And without giving me a chance to ask any further questions, he changed the subject.

"You ought to know more about Nice, Persis." He took my arm and began to lead me along the cart path that meandered between the farms. "The Old City, the only part of Nice with which we of the society need to concern ourselves, extends technically between the covered-over river that is called le Paillon, the Château, and the sea. The Old City has two quarters – the first around the Hôtel de Ville and the Préfecture of Police. It was once crisscrossed by seventeenth-century streets where we now have the site of the famous flower market."

An expert change of subject, I mused. "The French love to cover over city rivers. Rennes, for example."

"Did you know that Bonaparte lived at number six on the street that's named after him? That was in 1794, when he was a general of artillery and just before he was arrested after the fall of Robespierre. What a history. Nice had been *rattachá* to France only the previous year."

This was heavy stuff. I was surprised at his knowledge. Yet it was logical that any member of a society to restore the old parts of an ancient city would know its history by heart.

"Nice was restored to Sardinia in 1814," he

continued, "and only returned to France by a plebiscite in 1860. And by the way, Napoleon – do I bore you?"

He must have seen the glaze in my eye. But we artists are nothing if not game. "Never. Please go on."

"Then you'll be amused to know that he came back to Nice in 1796 as commander in chief of the army of Italy and stayed in a house in the rue St.-François-de-Paule, in front of the Opéra. He married Josephine several days later."

I, who can barely remember my own birthday (why, now that I think of it, would I want to?), was duly impressed. "You have a phenomenal memory."

He laughed for the first time. "Not really. You can get it out of any book. And anyway, we members of the board repeat all this a dozen times a week when we're soliciting help or funds."

He said it lightly, but I was pleased. It proved to me that the board members were serious people, interested in more than eating and drinking and capering about.

On the other hand, the more Guarnieri talked, the more I began to feel that I was being made a fool of – very politely, very subtly, and very professionally. He was sending up smoke screens. I was sure of it.

First of all, he was definitely uneasy — and why should he be? Secondly, I'd overheard bits and pieces of his passionate conversation with the farmer earlier, and they hadn't been talking about the landings. They had been talking about the Gestapo.

Chapter 10

It was 8:00 A.M. when my telephone did its mysterious musical number.

My first thought was that someone from the board was calling. Then I remembered that they all had flown off to Ibiza to interview an architect who was supposed to be a genius at restoring ancient buildings. Their time between meals was spent on projects like that.

"Madame Willum?" The voice was very polite, very correct.

"Yes."

"I am Albert Eude, and I am telephoning on the part of the mayor."

He was back. Things were about to move forward.

"The mayor would like to see you this morning. Are you free?"

Was I free? "Of course. What time?"

"Eleven. We will send a car for you."

"That won't be necessary. I can drive myself. I have a car."

"I'm sorry, we must insist." He was very firm.

"We will, as I said, send a car for you. Eleven o'clock. And the mayor regrets that he has not been in touch with you sooner."

"It's quite all right. I —"

He interrupted. "There is just one thing. The mayor wishes to keep this interview private. You are not to discuss it, or any future meetings, without his permission."

The mayor wasn't the first client to make eccentric requests. If that was the way he wanted it, it was all right with me. "Certainly. Understood."

But he had already hung up; the mayor's representative was a man of few words.

He was also as good as his word. Promptly at eleven the bell at my front gate sounded. A man in a business suit was waiting. He did not look like a businessman. Neither did he look like a chauffeur. He looked like a bodyguard, all muscle.

With a couple of grunts and no smiles he indicated that I was required to sit in front beside him, and I did. There was no conversation. In that sense the trip reminded me of my initial drive with Longhi, except that this time we were going the opposite way — at least, I think we were — in the general direction of Cagnes. But then we appeared to turn sharply back into the hills, toward Nice again. It was an uphill-downhill drive amid unfamiliar streets

78

and byways that left me so confused I lost all sense of direction. Doubtless it was planned that way.

We must have cruised around for an hour because I heard the cannon go off at the Château high above the Old Port, signifying to the populace that it was noon and time for everyone to rush home to eat and drink. Only then was our tour of Nice over. We turned so sharply off the road that we almost ran into the stone gates we then plunged through.

We lurched down a bumpy drive bordered by untamed undergrowth. The villa at the end had the air of having given up all hope as it rotted, abandoned, in the midst of scraggly, dispirited palms and unpruned fruit trees.

But the front door opened smartly enough the minute the Peugeot stopped, and another unlikely-looking man in a business suit motioned us in.

"Hurry. He's waiting."

It was a different world inside the villa. The interior was as luxurious as the exterior was dilapidated, shimmering with tapestries, ormolu clocks, gold candlesticks, painted vases, gilded chairs, and ornately framed paintings by lesser-known contemporary artists. I saw a gold harp tucked in among pots of flowers blooming in a corner.

It astonished me. "The mayor plays?"

"Decoration," the business suit replied rather scornfully. Mayors don't play the harp on earth, he implied, and possibly not in heaven either.

I was led swiftly past a series of ornate rooms and into a glass-enclosed breakfast room, where black and red lacquer chairs with gold dragon arm supports surrounded a glass-topped table whose pedestal was a priceless Oriental vase.

Jules Ribot was seated there like some exotic potentate.

I recognized him immediately. He looked like his photographs, only better. Very tan. Close-cropped gray hair hugging a nicely shaped head. Deep-set black eyes. Strong nose. Passionate lips. And the famous flashing smile.

It was flashing now. "Ah, Mrs. Willum. At last." He did not rise to greet me.

"Mr. Mayor. Also at last."

"Excuse me if I do not get up to shake hands . . . a slight indisposition . . ."

He was wearing spotless white shorts, canvas shoes, and a white Egyptian cotton shirt unbuttoned to the navel. Across his chest, below his left shoulder, strips of gauze bandage held in place with adhesive were clearly visible. The indisposition.

"Welcome to my 'safe house.' It sounds very dramatic, doesn't it?" He looked down at the strips of bandage. "You might as well know in the beginning. Somebody was a lousy shot. Naturally I tell you this in strictest confidence; if we're to work together, we must have confidence in one another." He grinned at me as if we were coconspirators in some delightful plot, and I understood at once the secret of his charm: He made me feel immediately special.

"Strictest confidence," I promised. "So it's true — someone did try to kill you?"

"Not very successfully, luckily. But that's between us. As far as the rest of the world is concerned, I'm out of town, taking a cure, pursuing a love affair, or being 'done over' — take your pick. Personally I don't care what they believe — the wound is comparatively minor, and I'll recover — but I'm going to stay right here in this house, lying low, until I'm better healed or somebody tips his hand or both." He put on the dark glasses that lay beside him on the table, but not before I caught the chill in his eyes.

I noted that he flinched as he moved.

"You're quite safe here?"

"Quite. Let me list my *gardes du corps:* two former gendarmes, several professional marksmen, and an inspector of police. Even Albert, my major-domo, was a colonel in the army. I couldn't be in better hands. They've been with me from the start. And they've been blooded."

"You mean —"

81

"There have been episodes. Last year, for example, there was an unfortunate affair. They do not hesitate to shoot. They are professionals of the highest caliber."

Then how, I wondered, had someone managed to wound him?

He knew what I was thinking. "That shooting was a fluke. There was a diversion, a distraction. An auto accident. It looked serious — very cleverly done. My men thought the accident was the main event, but it wasn't. For the first time they blew it. But my safe house lives up to its name. A veritable armed camp."

"Good. Then we will work here? When do we start the portrait?"

"I want to talk about that. I'd like to begin at once if it's all right with you. I have a deadline — all of life is a deadline when you're in politics. Furthermore, I don't want to waste a moment of the chance to be in your attractive company. How long will the portrait take?"

I could feel myself color at his compliment, slight though that compliment was. "I have a deadline, too, Mr. Mayor. I've already been here six days, counting today. I have a job back home, and my employer won't let me stay away forever. Ten days for the portrait, if we work every day and if I can leave my materials here. A sitting of one hour a day and permission to stay on for an hour or so afterward to paint on my own." If all went well, that is. But it should. He would be a good subject.

"Perfect. Couldn't be better."

"Begin tomorrow then?"

"Tomorrow. But there is one thing: The exact time will always be different. You'll be notified first thing in the morning each day. Precautionary measure, lest you be followed. The first rule of safety is never to stick to a pattern. Vary your course, always. Never drive the same streets. And you're to tell no one what you're doing or where you're going or that I'm here in Nice."

"You have my word." Actually, it sounded rather exciting.

"There is one more thing." The black eyes behind the dark glasses seemed to be drilling holes in me. Then the famous smile flashed on, like the sun rising. "I need your help. Someone has tried to kill me, and I intend to find out who. I have no intention of dying on somebody else's time schedule — not even on God's, if I can help it. I want you to find out everything you can about the board and keep me informed. We checked with Interpol when you were proposed for this job, and they mentioned that you'd worked with the FBI on a couple of occasions. They didn't specify what, but it's obvious you know a thing or two. I have reason to suspect the board — never mind why, just believe me. Keep your ears and eyes open, find out everything you can, and report to me, will you?"

I searched frantically, in my surprise, for something to say. The best I could manage was, "Suspect them of what?"

"Trying to kill me. I realize it sounds paranoid. Obviously I have enemies; every politician does. But you'll just have to trust me on this. I have my reasons to be suspicious, believe me."

I couldn't believe him. It was too outrageous. Those nice, harmless people? People with a cause? People who went around making things beautiful? People devoted to pleasure?

Never.

But he had unquestionably been shot. It couldn't hurt to humor him if it made him happy. "All right. But it was probably some fanatic or some nut." The society didn't have any nuts, unless you counted Robin Wilson and the princess and Guarnieri with his passion for old war machines. But they were harmless. In fact, the only nut in the vicinity might be the mayor himself. No . . . that wasn't fair. A bullet had proved that he wasn't.

"I promise you there are no assassins in the collection of *bons vivants* that currently employ me, Mr. Mayor, but I'll keep my eyes and ears open, as you ask."

He leaned back and put his hands behind his head, smiling happily. "Thank you. Until tomorrow?"

"Tomorrow."

I had no intention of spying on my friends. But he had charm. There was no denying it.

So how could it hurt to indulge him — even if I was only pretending?

Chapter 11

Before the day was over, I had reason to suspect that the mayor's fantasies might not be so bizarre after all.

I was to take tea that afternoon with the Clough-Whites. Like me, they had not gone with the rest to Ibiza. Like me, they couldn't afford it. The idea of taking tea with them in the heat of midsummer didn't exactly send me into ecstasies, but Nicole had implied that it was more or less *de rigueur* to accept, so here I was.

Their house was named Lilac Cottage, presumably in honor of the deep purple French lilacs that drooped in heavy clusters from every available inch of the modest pink building. Like its name, everything about Lilac Cottage was relentlessly English. The living room featured a gas fireplace. The walls were papered with reproductions of English flowers. The furniture blazed with a variety of cheery chintzes. The miniature garden was clipped and hedged. An astounding collection of firearms was mounted conspicuously throughout.

The Clough-Whites stood side by side to greet me, with the practiced correctness of civil servants who had survived countless official receptions in countless far-flung outposts of the empire.

"Do come in." His smile revealed yellow teeth that were a patriotic testament to years of neglect during service abroad. "You'll find that we live very simply. But comfortably."

"We love our dear snuggery," she chimed in. "A little bit of England on the Riviera, we always say. And so comforting, after all those years in Nigeria and the Sudan and India . . ."

"And Italy, my dear. Don't forget Italy."

"Oh, yes . . . Italy. But those were not the best of times, were they?" She didn't elaborate, seeming to assume that I understood. I racked my brain. What had happened in Italy that would involve British civil servants? I came up dry.

He was now fussing about at a bar which had been installed atop a battered old campaign chest in the corner. "A small libation, perhaps? To celebrate your visit?"

I scanned the selection of bottles. Gin or sherry. "I think not, thanks."

"Sun's over the yardarm, you know. Up to you." He poured himself a generous gin and hoisted his glass. "The queen!"

I lowered myself onto the rose-covered chintz of a sofa whose springs had long since surrendered. "The queen," I said, hoisting an imaginary glass of my own.

The temperature was hovering around ninety. Nonetheless, a full and lavish English tea had been set out, complete with a formidable array of small sandwiches, cakes, and chipped Spode china.

"Lovely service," I told them politely.

"We love beautiful things." He refilled his glass.

The steam from my teacup rose languidly and mingled with the steam of the non-air-conditioned room.

Mrs. Clough-White — Elizabeth — arranged her sensibly clad feet perfectly side by side and pulled her ubiquitous print dress down farther over her plumpish knees. "We both have a special feeling for beauty. Art, you might say, is our hobby."

"We've lived everywhere, almost, and seen everything," he explained, wiping his mustache with a linen tea napkin. The mustache had a greenish rusty tinge, like metal left too long outdoors. Clough-White, now that I thought about it, had a slightly rusty tinge himself. Perhaps it came with the civil servant territory.

He now began a long, rambling account of the places where he had served, punctuated at regular intervals by helpful asides from his wife. I quickly lost the thread. Blame it on the heat, the steaming tea, the airless room.

"I was with Monty's Eighth," I heard at one point.

"More tea? Of course you do, my dear."

"Moved on afterwards. Other branches of the service. Here and there. Love it here. Marvelous climate, nice people, good food."

"He loves good food."

"Crazy about art wherever we were. Thrilled to know you. Greatly admire your work. Must have art around one, right? Stuff of life and all that. Can't be done without, really. Oh, yes, very important."

"Important," she echoed.

They were so sincere.

But I didn't see any sign of art in their house. Shouldn't there be at least a reproduction of something? Surely they could afford that much?

"Where did you go to school? Whom did you study under? Did you bring any books on your work? We'd so love to see them. Tell us about your life. Where did you grow up? Have you any brothers or sisters?"

It was a quiz. I wondered if all visitors underwent this catechism.

"You must forgive us . . . it's just that we're so thrilled to have a famous artist in our house that we can't help wanting to know all about you. Because we love art as we do, it's a great treat . . . like having the queen or some other member of royalty. Because, you see, to us artists are like royalty. You must forgive us . . ."

By now I had pulled out my trusty fan and was using it vigorously. They seemed to be maddeningly composed and cool despite the heat and their strenuous questioning.

He poured a third drink. She poured more tea. They both downed cakes and sandwiches as if they didn't expect to eat for a year. Maybe it was because they wouldn't be dining out tonight. The group that paid their way was in Ibiza and wouldn't return until tomorrow.

"When we're back home, we spend hours at the Victoria and Albert, you know," he told me.

"Oh, really? I've been dying to see the newly acquired Beardsley drawings. Beardsley — imagine anyone so talented dying at twenty-six years of age. Like Keats."

"Indeed. So sad," she agreed. "So very sad. We do so love art."

"You cannot possibly imagine the hours we've spent at the Tate." He was peering at me in a most intense manner, like someone who needed glasses to see something right under his nose. But he didn't wear glasses.

I don't know what came over me. It must have been the hot room and the hot tea. Or maybe it was resentment of all the questioning. I detest being questioned because I detest having to talk about myself.

"The Tate . . ." I said. "Don't you love the Blakes?"

"Oh, we adore them."

"And the superb Turners?"

"Superb!"

"The Constables, too?"

"Magnificent."

"And how do you like the sixteenth- and seventeenth-century collection? Don't you agree that the little panel by Edward Everett Simms is the best of them all?"

"We certainly do. It's the best we've ever seen, in fact. Wonderful."

I stood up. I excused myself.

I made my way firmly past the tea table, the campaign chest, the mounted elephant and other guns, the chintz-covered furniture, and out the door. Then I made my way past the hedged garden and drooping lilacs to my car. Clough-White flew wingman. His wife came rushing after.

"Do wait. A present." She caught up and pressed a sticky object upon me. "Our own honey from our own hives."

It had a handwritten label across the front:

"Lilac Cottage Honey." The jar stuck to my fingers.

"Thank you."

I climbed into my car and tromped on the gas pedal. The Ford, like a horse unexpectedly spurred by a rider it had always considered a friend, leaped forward with injured dignity.

Behind me I heard them call out, "Remember . . . you're welcome anytime. We loved our little chat."

In my rear-view mirror I could see them standing there, watching my departure. They were hand in hand, the perfect vision of two devoted retirees. It all was so very British: the house, the garden, the tea party, the conversation, even the honey.

Too perfect perhaps? Almost a caricature?

All that talk about art. And not even a picture postcard on the wall. The intense, relentless questioning — so unBritish.

There was something else. The Tate didn't have a sixteenth-century painting by an artist named Edward Everett Simms. Edward Everett Simms was my friend on the FBI art squad, and he was definitely not a painter in this or any other century.

It was strange. Not strange enough to report to Ribot, but strange enough to put in my own private mental computer and store for future reference.

Chapter 12

The sittings began the next morning, exactly seven days after my arrival in Nice.

The mayor was waiting in the same breakfast room, wearing his same uniform of white shorts, white shirt, bandages, and canvas shoes. It was all right with me.

"I've decided to paint you in white," I told him.

"No three-piece suit, like a president of the republic?" he joked. The incumbent president was never seen in anything else.

"No. You're a good subject. You interest me — as a painting, I mean."

"That's too bad. I wouldn't mind interesting you in some other way." It wasn't offensive, just gallant.

"I've spent the last week learning everything there is to know about the man named Ribot."

He frowned. "I sincerely hope not everything."

"Everything I could. It's important for my work to understand you."

He smiled his charming smile. "And do you? If so, you know me better than I know myself. Do you approve of what you've learned?" The tone was flirtatious, playful.

"You'll do, I think." I smiled back and began to set up my canvas and lay out my paints. "Anyway, I've decided how to portray you, and that's half the battle."

"And how will that be?"

"A dark man, very dark. A white shirt, open at the neck. A man who might have lived in any century."

I never begin to paint without having some point of view toward my subject. That point of view sometimes changes while I'm working, but I always begin somewhere. This time I was beginning with a powerful, dynamic personality, a man who was headed for a place in history. He was not just the mayor of a major European city; he was a man of destiny. He believed it. Many others in France believed it.

Rather to my surprise, I did, too. He was capable, I felt, of achieving whatever goal he chose.

"A man of any century," he repeated. Obviously the image pleased him.

"A strong man. But a man who also has a genuine appreciation of beauty. And of history, obviously, since you support the cause of the society in restoring and protecting the Old City."

He leaned forward, wincing slightly as he did. "About the society . . . have you discovered anything?"

"They've been in Ibiza." I didn't mention my tea with the Clough-Whites; there wasn't really any reason. "And now, Mr. Mayor, I must begin to work. I'm not the kind of portraitist who carries on a sparkling conversation with the subject while she's painting. . . . I'm the silent, concentrating type, I'm afraid. So if you don't mind actually, you can work, too. I won't even notice, I'll be concentrating so hard."

"Wonderful. I'm a thousand years behind on everything, as you may imagine."

He summoned Albert, who appeared immediately, armed with folders and papers and telephones to be plugged in. Within seconds the breakfast room was transformed into an office and the mayor and his major-domo were at work.

I began to sketch preliminary lines on the primed canvas. I already had the mood of Ribot's likeness in mind. This was a complex man; therefore, my approach would be simple. I would approach my subject in the spirit of scientific purity. Like Velásquez. Not just copying nature but deliberately trying to bring to it a magnified simplicity from which every intrusive detail has been removed, presenting an intensified version of the subject that forces the portrait to speak for itself and the viewer to form his own opinion.

I would paint him in an open white shirt, like a king at rest or a Spanish grandee at leisure. Other than that, no hint of time or place. No historical framework. No clues.

Obviously Ribot was a man of many facets. It was one of the reasons for his success. So, I would let the viewer choose for himself the Ribot he preferred. I was already beginning to discover a favorite Ribot of my own.

B. B. Benezit was the first to check in. She did it in person, ringing the bell at my gate in the early afternoon.

"Can a weary traveler find something cool to drink at this house?"

I was astonished to see her. "Aren't you back early?"

"A little. I returned this morning, and I called you; but you didn't answer your phone. Where were you?"

"Around. When do the rest arrive?"

"On the late-afternoon plane. We're all due for dinner on Franck's yacht, remember?"

I'd forgotten. Franck was eminently forgettable. "Will they be back in time?"

"Probably. He's a big contributor. But you

never know with them."

She looked awful. "How did you happen to come back before the rest?"

"That's easy. Robin didn't come, of course; he's not board. And at the last minute neither did my wonderful husband. He said he was taking a later flight, but he never showed up. I was worried. So back I came this morning."

Visions of the florid, overweight Mustard succumbing to a heart attack rushed into my head.

She must have read my mind because she said, "Don't worry. There isn't any corpse. He's around somewhere. Actually I thought you might have seen him. Was he here, by any chance?"

"Why would he be here?"

"Why not? He likes attractive people of any sex. Aren't you going to let me in?"

"Of course." I hurried to unlock the gate. "How about some iced coffee? I actually have ice."

"Perfect."

She didn't exactly look her best. The kohl she used to emphasize her black eyes was smeared, and either it or lack of sleep had painted dark shadows that reached all the way down to her round cheeks – cheeks that were pale today. The lipstick on the insolent mouth was slightly awry, as if it had been applied through a curtain of tears, although I couldn't imagine Benezit crying.

Even her clothes were mussed. I wondered if she'd slept in them. Most unusual for Benezit to look unkempt; her studied chic was one of the reasons she always seemed more French than the French.

"Good grief, Persis," she said as I let her through the gate, "do you mean to tell me that Nicole finally had it fixed?"

I hadn't the least notion what she meant. "What?"

"The gate, of course."

"Why?"

"It's not sticking, that's why. I fought my way in here a million times when Robin was in residence; we all did. And Nicole would never fix it. All it needed was a new hinge or two. How did you do it?"

I hadn't said a word to Nicole. But now that B.B. had pointed it out, I realized that the gate had indeed opened smoothly and silently for the first time, without the usual struggle. One of her slaves must have fixed it that morning while I was out painting the mayor.

"I'm just lucky, I guess. Come inside."

She followed me upstairs, still talking. "I suppose he was with Robin — or spying on him. You can't imagine what it's like being married to a man like Mustard. He's always infatuated with somebody. Actually I think it would have been a relief to find he'd stayed behind to see you. Lesser of two evils. I never dreamed when I married him –" She stopped abruptly and changed the subject. "I don't suppose I could change that order to a whiskey?"

"Don't have any. Kir? Pastis? Sorry, no tea."

"Thank God for that," she said fervently. "I gather you've been subjected to the ritual tea at Lilac Cottage. Frightful, isn't it? Kir, please . . . a big one."

"Well," I admitted, "tea at Lilac Cottage isn't your usual day on the Côte d'Azur. Still, they claim to be art enthusiasts." Certainly she would know something about that.

But if she did, she wasn't talking. "Isn't *everyone* here? Everybody claims to be an expert. This great picture . . . that great collection – it's all I hear. They're telling *me,* and I'm the one who's supposed to be the authority. Crazy. By the way, not to change the subject or anything, but who's the good-looking chap on the opposite balcony?"

She was downing her kir in rapid gulps, as if eager to be on her way now that she was satisfied Mustard wasn't in residence.

I saw that my neighbor had appeared and was working on his plants. "Somebody who rents from Nicole."

"That explains it. I thought he looked famil-iar. I saw him nod to her a couple of times downtown, and I asked then ... There can never be too many extra men around. She said he's not one of us. Here on business of some probably not-too-attractive kind. Not in our group, so I guess he must work, if you know what I mean. Keeps to himself, she said." She sighed. "Too bad. I like lots of new people. I've become used to group living since I joined the board. It's comforting, like belonging to a herd or a flock or a pack."

"Speaking of Nicole, what did you mean the other day about her history of love affairs?"

Benezit was now on her way back downstairs, moving in swift fits and starts. She did every-thing in swift fits and starts, like someone eternally on the verge of a crisis of nerves. "Oh, that was centuries before Mustard and I arrived on the scene. And one doesn't ask. Not done. Still, there are always rumors. And the one about her is that she knew Ribot long before the society was formed."

To my surprise I felt a small twinge of jealousy. Just a small one. But still. Was I beginning to feel proprietary about Ribot?

"Friends?" I asked hopefully.

She pulled open the gate, which didn't resist. She produced an enormous pair of dark glasses and plunked them on her bold little nose.

"Lovers." For the first time today she offered her gamine grin. "Red-hot lovers."

She blew me a kiss and shut the gate.

B. B. Benezit's surprise visit left me feeling disturbed. Not a big, crashing kind of disturbed, but one riddled with little pinpricks of unease.

Was it possible that she could believe her bloated, booze-soaked husband had stayed behind because of me, that I would let him? I suppose he must have been attractive once or she wouldn't have married him. Flashes of a younger, more presentable Mustard occasionally shone through, but they were merely flashes – never enough to make him palatable. Poor Benezit, she must care for him still.

Why *had* Mustard stayed behind? And Robin? It had been my impression that Robin Wilson, although not a member of the board and thus not technically included in the Ibiza trip, had been invited by Nicole to accompany them. But I remembered someone saying that he had changed his mind about going. Why had *he* stayed behind? Had Mustard really forsworn Ibiza to be with Wilson – or to spy on him? If it was to spy on him, what was Wilson doing?

And there was something else. How could Benezit and Mustard afford the life they were living as part of the not-so-idle rich of the Côte d'Azur? Beautiful clothes, trips to Ibiza (and soon to Paris), endless meals in the most expensive restaurants — how did they manage?

The more I thought about it, the more uneasy I became.

Was it possible that Mustard's once-upon-a-time best seller was still producing royalties? There'd been nothing from Benezit in the last several years. How, then, did they support their expensive style of living?

Why was I so suspicious? Were Ribot's suspicions getting to me?

There was one thing I could do: I could satisfy myself once and for all about Mustard's book. Of course, it must still be in print; what other explanation could there be? The French, after all, unlike Americans, are avid readers. Wherever you see them — on planes, the metro, in restaurants, on park benches — they are reading books. So it was possible the book was still selling. But I had to know.

The biggest bookshop I'd seen in Nice was just down from the flower market. If *Love Lives of the Superrich* still existed, it would have it.

Satisfying myself didn't take long. I was down in the Old City in a few minutes and parking in the cavernous special area beneath the market, which was swarming with its usual crowds of people buying flowers of all kinds.

The French love affair with flowers is second only to their love affair with food and wine and breakneck speed.

The bookstore, too, was jammed. Citizens were buying books as if they were shortly to be declared illegal.

But there was no book by James Gallop Mustard. Nor had the salesperson heard of it.

All the way back up to Mount Boron my mind kept wandering. I hated the things I was thinking.

Nicole de Plessis and the mayor. A bizarre affair between Mustard and Wilson. Benezit spying on her husband.

It was a whole chain of nasty thoughts. A chain I'd better break.

So when the moment came to turn off for L'Oasis, I kept right on going. I'd been promising myself ever since my arrival to visit the top of Mount Boron. There were still a couple of hours of daylight left, and my sketchbook was with me. Normally I am terrified of heights, but when I had first mentioned being afraid to go to the top of Mount Boron, they had laughed at me.

"High?" Very amused. "Don't you know the crest is called the plateau? Mount Boron is really a sort of mini-mountain. It's true the sides are steep, but the top has been worn down through the centuries so that it's like a great big saucer or a soccer field. You'll love it once you're there. There are wonderful views from the various walks."

So now I turned my car's nose upward and headed for the top, careful not to look out the side window. The precipice that dropped down to the sea commanded respect.

At the top I parked in a small square. It was like being in a miniature village. There were one or two villas, a small hotel, a large fountain, and splendid views of Cap Ferrat all the way to the Old Port.

An infinite variety of children was kicking soccer balls around the square and an equally infinite variety of dogs was enthusiastically chasing after them: dachshunds, poodles, papillons, pointers, setters, Pekes, Alsatians, and just plain mutts, all of them barking.

There was also a marvelous assortment of women in sleeveless cotton dresses and spindly-legged men in shorts.

And once again there was Mario Guarnieri deep in conversation, this time with not one but two elderly men.

Chapter 13

"Mario . . . you're back!"

The scent of eucalyptus was everywhere. And there was a great fluttering of pigeons vying with one another to sample the fountain's clear water.

He muttered something, and his two companions shook hands quickly and retreated.

"The architect was a disaster," Guanieri said. "The trip was a waste of time. We're all home. I'm about to walk the kinks out of my airplane legs."

"So you all came running home. I don't blame you. This seems to be a popular place for walking. May I join you?"

He didn't look thrilled. "Well . . ." There was a pause. Finally he took my arm. "The paths are all mapped out on this sign. Which do you choose?"

Obviously he didn't want my company. But I didn't care. I was curious. What was he doing up here? Had he really come just for a walk?

I voted for something called the Sentier des

Crêtes (because it meant the top and I was now feeling overconfident and anxious to prove my mettle), and we set off, dodging children and dogs and bowing to strolling families as we passed.

The blue waters below us seemed to stretch into infinity, with faraway sailboats looking stationary on the gentle swells. Sleek power-boats cut silver arrows through the sea. Far off was Africa; the thought thrilled me. And all around — sprinkled on the hills that went down to the water — I could see occasional gleams of roofs or swimming pools.

"Our houses, some of them," Mario told me.

"Gorgeous."

"To your left is the harbor of Villefranche, where Franck keeps his yacht. His mail is sent to the Welcome Hotel on the quay; he picks it up there. It's convenient, and there's a great restaurant at his fingertips."

I thought of Franck and shuddered.

A group of runners thudded past, their eyes fixed on the path ahead, their brown legs pumping in unison. They were like perfectly conditioned horses, not even breathing hard.

One of them was my neighbor. He was by far the oldest of the runners who flashed by, yet he was not only keeping up but leading.

"That man in front is my neighbor."

"Oh? Must be in great condition," Guarnieri

said. "Anyone running up here has to have good legs. It's a challenge. They like to test themselves against the uphill, downhill topography."

"Suppose you toppled off the path? I think I'd prefer the esplanade."

He was staring after the running men. "They all look in peak condition, don't they?" They rounded a curve in the path and disappeared. "Just watching them expend all that energy makes me feel out of shape. Let's sit down and admire the sights, shall we? I'm exhausted by osmosis."

A grandmother and grandfather walked slowly past the bench we had appropriated, followed by two small children and a large red setter.

"That's Nicole's house directly below us, Persis."

The house itself wasn't really visible because of the trees, but the pool was.

"Have you heard from the mayor yet?"

I'm not a very good liar. I leaned down and pretended to shake a pebble out of my shoe. "Have *you* heard anything, Mario? I really should be getting to work. I can't stay here forever."

"Nobody believes the assassination story. One of the papers reported that he'd been seen at a Swiss health spa. Frenchmen do it all the time;

he's undoubtedly getting himself in shape for the coming campaign. He'll be back in a few days for the Bataille de Fleurs, you can be sure of it. Dead or alive. With the TV and the press all over the place he wouldn't dare miss such a golden opportunity for a public appearance."

It couldn't be soon enough to suit me. I hated the idea of sneaking around, painting in secret, and being expected to spy on my friends. And yet – I had to admit it – there was something exciting about it, too. Presidential campaigns. Unsuccessful assassination attempts. Unanswered questions.

I wanted to get off the subject of the mayor for fear of giving something away. It was absurd to imagine any of the board could wish him ill, but still . . .

"How is your paper coming along, Mario?"

He seemed bewildered. "Paper?"

"The one about the Landings – the one you told me about. Maybe I'll be here on Liberation Day, August twenty-eighth, when you give it? Who knows. At the rate things are going . . ."

"I'm not sure what you're talking about, Persis."

It was only a conversation on a summers' day. "All those people you talk to in the countryside. The maquis and all that."

He turned away from me and stared out to sea. Maybe he was trying to see all the way to Africa. "You think you'll still be here then?"

"Well, the mayor isn't back yet. So who knows?"

He concentrated on the horizon. Morocco, I decided, he's trying to see Morocco. And with the concentration he was bringing to the task, I wouldn't have been surprised if he succeeded.

"So maybe I'll be lucky enough to be here."

He made a strangled sound, halfway between despair and anger. "I misled you a little bit, Persis. There is no address. So if you're still here on Liberation Day, don't be disappointed."

"But you said — "

"I know." Impatient.

"Those people you talked to?" Didn't anyone ever tell the truth around here?

"Something else entirely."

"Really?"

He finally looked at me, and his eyes were soft and sorry in his broken face. "I lied to you. I'm writing a book about the war in this region."

"Why didn't you say so?" I was surprised.

"I was afraid you would laugh. I'm a race driver, not a writer."

"What difference does that make? You're an expert on the war."

"I don't know. Maybe I'll use yet another name."

"*Yet* another . . ."

109

"Let me tell you something: No one here is what he seems. The whole Côte d'Azur is composed of mirages."

I thought he was joking. He often was. "For example?"

But he wasn't. "For example, my name isn't Guarnieri. That's a professional name, taken because it has class. Distinction. Like the violin. My real name is so common on the Côte d'Azur nobody would remember me."

"What is your real name?"

"It doesn't matter. That was years ago. I'm Guarnieri now."

"I like it. It's soft. It suits you."

"But I am not soft. Never believe it. Especially not with my enemies."

I wanted to laugh. The thought of Mario with enemies was as ludicrous as the thought of his being hard with anyone.

The two small children and the red setter returned just then, the boy bearing the soccer ball that is the natural appendage of all French children in summer. He immediately threw it over the side of the path. The setter bounded after it. Both came to a halt against a rock at what had to be the last possible resting place before disaster.

The two children turned and stared expectantly at Guarnieri. Guarnieri stared at the rapid descent of hill. He sighed. Then he stood

110

up and, with the utmost calm, started down the precipice, rock by rock.

I couldn't watch. All my terror of heights roared back and overwhelmed me. It was impossible for me to follow his progress. Surely he would fall. I felt weak. Dizzy.

I tried to find something — anything — that would serve as an anchor for my vision — something, anything — that would be familiar and steadying. Nicole's pool.

It was clearly visible below us. Blue and solid.

And there were two people down there. They hadn't been there before, but they were there now, their figures so far away, so tiny, that they were like stick figures in a naïf's painting. Engaged in a drama that threatened to upstage Guarnieri and his rescue.

Nicole and Robin Wilson. Face-to-face, stage center, delivering their lines. The lighting was perfect: Her black hair gleamed; his gold jewelry glistened. Only by the attitudes of their two small bodies could you tell that there was tension between them, but it was there as clearly as if you could hear them speak.

I stared, fascinated. It was like being on the balcony of the Mark Hellinger Theater and watching the actors onstage far below. Not quite like eavesdropping — they were too far away to hear. More like watching a silent film without captions.

A confrontation. Two antagonists face-to-face. They leaned toward each other. Suddenly she struck him; even from so far away I could see that it was hard. For a moment they stood very still. Then she threw herself against him and began to kiss his face, his eyes, his bare chest.

He stood rigid, submitting.

She said something. And as suddenly as she had struck him, he struck back, returning the compliment with a blow that sent her staggering.

Four frozen instants. Then they quit the stage, each in a different direction.

It was over. Persis Willum, unwilling audience of one, could now leave the balcony.

But there was someone else. He was on the path below ours, the Sentier de Nice, and he was standing still, watching. Longhi's chauffeur.

There had been, after all, an audience of two.

"Persis, lend a hand, please."

Guarnieri was six very vertical steps below me. The soccer ball was tucked under one arm, the other was stretched toward me. "Wouldn't you think the damn dog would retrieve it?"

"Mouth's not big enough." There was a tree next to me. I put one arm around it, closed my eyes, and reached down for Guarnieri. I felt the steel of his grasp.

The dog was standing on the same small ledge as Mario, barking furiously at him, as it had been barking during the entire rescue.

"Damn dog," I heard Mario say.

I felt the pressure of Guarnieri's hand increase. I heard scrambling. I felt him release my hand.

I opened my eyes.

Guarnieri was in front of me with the soccer ball still beneath his arm. Bits and pieces of leaves and twigs clung all over him, and his immaculate white trousers were torn at the knee.

He handed the ball to the little boy, who marched off, little girl and dog in tow, the latter pausing for a final bark before departing.

"I'm too old for mountain climbing." But I noticed that, like my neighbor who had pounded by, he wasn't even breathing hard. "Why were you hanging on to that tree. Afraid I was going to pull you off the path? If worst came to worst, I'd have dropped the ball, silly girl."

"I know." I felt ashamed.

Guarnieri try to pull me off the path? The kindly writer of books and rescuer of balls?

I had better get a grip on myself. Paranoia was apparently setting in.

Chapter 14

The invitation to dine on Anton Franck's yacht had included all of us, but I was the first to arrive.

The yacht's launch had picked me up and ferried me quickly across the small harbor. It was nine o'clock when I boarded the *Miranda*.

She was a lovely craft, all graceful lines and polished teak. Franck was waiting in the midst of glittering gold leaf mirrors, Oriental rugs, fine paintings, and crystal chandeliers.

"Am I early?" Where were the rest?

His two hands smothered mine, hotly. "We are alone. Change of plans at the last minute. The others will be along after dinner. It will give me a chance to get to know you."

I didn't like it. "But we all were supposed to be here for dinner. All of us." The only light came from crystal hurricane lamps that flickered romantically with each motion of the yacht as she rode the gentle swells.

"Why are you concerned? They had another engagement. They will be along. Champagne?"

"Perrier, please." I had never run a footrace around a yacht, and I was determined not to start now. A heady scent was being piped in through the air-conditioning system. I thought I recognized Estée and wondered if it was a gift from the lady herself. There was also soft music, something with French lyrics — very seductive.

"We'll dine on deck under the stars," he said. "The view is wonderful. You can see the coast all the way to St.-Trop."

I ought to be safe through dinner; he'd need someone to serve, I thought. And after? If the group didn't arrive, it looked as if I'd be swimming back to the Hôtel Welcome. At least, thank God, we weren't at sea.

"You like the *Miranda?*" He patted a spot beside him on a down-filled aquamarine silk sofa. I chose another chair. "I call her my bachelor boat."

I didn't like that either. "Should I ask why?"

"I'll show you after dinner. I'll give you the grand tour."

Not, I thought, unless you're also pumping chloroform through your air ducts. He looked more short, squat, and simian than ever. How, I wondered, could he possibly imagine anyone would want to tour his yacht with him? Nothing on earth could make such a trip attractive.

"You're Greek, Mr. Franck?"

"Call me Anton. Of course I'm Greek. Look, *Miranda* flies the Greek flag. Why do you ask?"

He could be anything. After all, we're all descended from apes. "I just wondered. Are you in shipping? All Greeks are in shipping, I believe." It's called making small talk.

"I am a citizen of the world. I am retired. I have been in many things, in my day." He reached out to pat my knee. I moved to another chair.

"You are married?" It wouldn't hurt to remind him if he was.

"Several times. At the moment, however, no. I am available."

I wondered if he expected me to fall upon him, weeping for joy.

"Well, I'm not — available, that is." It would be well to have the battle lines clearly drawn.

Not that it bothered him in the least. In fact, he laughed. "As to that, I know all about it. You're a young widow and perfectly available. We'll discuss it in detail after dinner." A white-coated black steward had appeared to announce dinner, and Franck led me out onto the deck, where a table had been set with gold plates and crystal wineglasses and large silver candelabra. He was right about the view. I felt safer. This close to the rail I could jump overboard and swim for it if I had to.

"I have planned this menu with you in mind

– something light, chic, luxurious, and beautiful, like you. A smoked Nordic salmon with a Graves to begin with. A quail consommé – I got the bird myself. A médaillon of veau with a Château Talbot St. Julien '77. . . ." His knee was already pressing mine under the table. I moved my knees, chair, and plate back an inch.

"Are you sure the rest are coming after dinner?"

He poured some wine. "What difference does it make? And if they don't come?"

"I'll have to leave, I'm afraid."

He looked at me over his wineglass. Everything about him turned suddenly hard and still as dead glacial rock. "As to that," he said, "you are wrong. You will stay. Don't try to play with me. Don't you think I know you've been watching, waiting for this? Oh, you want me, all right. And I happen also to find you attractive. It may be that we can strike a bargain here this night. What is the price for your . . . affection?"

I started to stand up, but he was around the table and pushing me back in my chair. "No, you will not go. Not until I say so. And when I say so."

I sank back, mostly because I couldn't stand his hairy paws on my shoulders. I felt their sweaty heat through the film of my light dress, and I imagined the sordid struggle that would follow if I resisted, a damp, degrading struggle while a million-dollar yacht swayed gently beneath us and the lights of the Riviera blinked gaily in the distance.

A rapid mental inventory of my escape choices was not promising. I could scream for help. But there wasn't another boat within earshot. Besides, screaming was embarrassing.

I could hit him over the head with something. That, at least, would give me pleasure. But with what? A slender silver candlestick? A goblet? Absurdly ineffective, almost guaranteed not to do the job.

No, my best weapon was talk. Keep the conversation going.

"I'm glad that you find me attractive," I said, very cool, very polite; sometimes good manners will keep a man at bay. "But I'm truly not interested."

"Skip the girlish games." He signaled to his steward, and the meal began. "Women always say no at first; it's an absurd ritual they insist on following. I have neither the time nor the temperament for such nonsense. I think you will find that I can teach you a thing or two; we'll see later. More wine, my dear? You'll find that we live well aboard this yacht. All the amenities. The best of everything. Do you like that scent? The music? You are lovely in the candlelight."

The meal began. The courses, which I barely touched, followed one another in stately, formal procession. What were we eating? What were we drinking? I had no idea.

The coffee and liqueur were served. Then I heard the discreet put-put of a departing launch and I understood that Franck and I were now alone. I was going to have to swim for it; there wasn't any doubt. Luckily it wasn't far.

Luckily I didn't have to.

"I hear music. You two dancing?"

It was Guy Longhi, all in white, like ectoplasm materializing. The *Miranda*'s departing launch had covered the sound of Longhi's boat arriving.

I didn't exactly crave Longhi, but at this moment I didn't exactly hate him either.

"I've come to take you home, Persis. Didn't Franck tell you? We're all going to Moustiers early tomorrow morning to select pottery for one of the restorations. We canceled dinner tonight because of it, and I promised Nicole to see that you got to bed at a decent hour."

Franck was enraged. "What are you doing here?"

"Collecting Persis, obviously. She's coming with the board tomorrow."

"You weren't supposed to be here tonight, Longhi." The words came slowly. He was so angry he had to force them out.

119

"Certainly true." Guy's hand was on my elbow, and his body was between me and Franck. He led me briskly across the deck and down the steps to the waiting motorboat he'd hired at the quay. "Sorry, old man. I guess you forgot about our Moustiers trip, didn't you? Or did you count on our canceling your invitation?"

"I won't forget this," Franck told him.

"I'm sure you won't." Longhi did not sound concerned.

And those were the last words I heard from the *Miranda* that night. They didn't seem any more bizarre than everything else I'd been hearing lately.

Longhi didn't speak until we were on the quay. "Do you have transportation here?"

"No. He sent a car."

"That figures. He would. Well, here's the Porsche."

I was looking at Longhi in a new way. "How did you happen to turn up just then?"

"When dinner was canceled, I got suspicious. Suppose you hadn't been notified? Pretty lady. Middle-aged lecher. Isolated boat. The scenario didn't seem quite sporting somehow. I guessed he might be up to something and phoned you. No answer. So I did the obvious. I didn't like the odds."

I was grateful. But at the same time my pride

was hurt. "I could have handled it."

"Of course you could. I'm certain you've had plenty of experience."

I wasn't exactly sure how he meant that remark. "Well, I *could* have handled it. Eventually."

"Probably. Except that Franck is not your ordinary civilized citizen. Far from it. I think someday you may find that his background is rather unsavory, and that the police know all about him. There are some pretty disreputable 'retired' characters living all over the place."

I felt properly chastened.

Longhi busied himself with the Porsche, and presently we were purring up the hill that leads out of Villefranche and onto the Lower Corniche. We raced silently along the road to Nice and then negotiated a sharp turn right, toward Mount Boron. Once again it was a silent ride.

Still, when we arrived at L'Oasis, I was almost sorry. Longhi's presence was comforting and agreeable. Tonight he seemed different — human.

He turned off the engine and pulled out a thin black cigar. "You permit?"

"Certainly." Actually I like the smell of tobacco; I'm a barely reformed smoker.

The cigar glowed briefly. He made no move to help me out of the car. I could see shadows of the palms tracing patterns against the walls of my villa. I could see tissue thin blossoms drifting in the garden, pale and fragile in the light over my door. It was very quiet. A black cat — one of the many wild ones that inhabited the vine-covered walls — raced across my walk and disappeared. It was pleasant sitting in the shadows, breathing in the scent of expensive leather and the even better scent of exotic flowers and the perfumed night. I couldn't see the stars from inside the car, but I knew they were there — jewels flickering in the inky sky.

I thought of home. Gull Harbor. I didn't miss it. Gull Harbor would be dank and humid now. Everyone who could afford it would have fled to Fisher's Island or Maine or Europe. Nice was paradise. Rather, it would be paradise if only I didn't feel like such a heel because I was doubting these people, who were being so very nice to me. Longhi, for example. He'd actually taken the trouble to extract me from Franck's hairy clutches. Some were undoubtedly odd (the Clough-Whites), slimy (Franck), mysterious (Guarnieri, Longhi, etc.), but none of them had given me reason to suspect that he or she was a potential murderer.

Longhi finally broke the companionable silence. "It's unfortunate that you haven't been able to begin your work."

It had been such a friendly moment that I almost told him the truth. But I caught myself in time. "I don't mind the wait. It's been very pleasant. You've all been very kind."

"Have you had any word from Ribot?"

"No, no." I was becoming adept at prevarication. "But it will only be a few more days if what they say is true. And, again, everyone has been so kind."

"True. But you must realize that you are dealing with expatriates from many different backgrounds and countries. They are here for a few months of the year. The rest of the time they are all over the world — New York, London, Rome, Paris, Alexandria ... you name it. In Nice they are bound together briefly by a single interest: the purely selfish one of preserving their way of life, which leads, fortunately, to good deeds like concern for the Old City. They stay on in the summer because that is the best time to get building and construction work done. Then most of them will vanish."

"What about Franck? What is his unsavory background you hinted at before?"

He turned to look at me, his blue eyes glinting briefly in the dark. "You must be aware by now that some of these people are not what they would have you believe. That's how it is on the Riviera, how it's always been."

"They seem nice enough — with a certain exception."

"That's how they wish to be perceived."

"It's perfectly normal, isn't it? Or are you trying to tell me something special?"

"I'm suggesting that you take nobody at face value. For example, Franck . . . a harmless, amorous Greek. Right? Wrong. He could be a criminal, living quietly under an assumed name, bothering no one —"

"Except me." I felt myself grow pale at the thought.

"Exactly. James Gallop Mustard . . . a best-selling author. Right? Wrong. An overweight, drunken failure who hasn't written a word in years. B. B. Benezit —"

But I didn't want to hear. "Franck . . . you mean, these people wine and dine with him —"

He was amused. "Not really. What they do is allow him to contribute vast sums of money to their cause. What do they care where the money comes from? Socialite fund raisers are the same all over the world. He's tolerated as long as he behaves . . . and gives generously."

The whole conversation began to seem surreal. "And Guy Longhi . . . what about him?"

He laughed. "Guy Longhi . . . is probably the worst of the lot. A fraud."

"Be serious. What do you do when you're not galloping around the Riviera with the group?"

"Nothing very interesting, I'm afraid. I'm a geologist. I travel here and there. I gather rock specimens. I write obscure articles for obscure journals. I travel to unheard-of, uninteresting places."

A geologist . . . that would explain his privacy, his introspection.

"Is that why, when you picked me up at the airport, you kept studying me as if I were a specimen? You didn't think I noticed, but I did."

He was surprised. "You're pretty observant. Well, why not tell you? It was because the mayor had asked for so many photos of you that my scientific mind asked, Why wouldn't *one* have been enough to show you were pretty? Why so many?"

"Was that all? Perhaps he just wanted to make sure. Photos sometimes lie."

"Perhaps."

He helped me out of the car and saw me through my silently opening gate. He bowed and stepped back into his beautiful green machine. He brought it to life. It sang out softly and then slipped down the hill and out of sight. I stayed at my gate, staring after its sleek, vanished form.

A geologist. A geologist with a chauffeur?

I unlocked the big front door and went upstairs to sit on my balcony and think.

Chapter 15

I don't know how many hours I sat staring into the night. I only know that it was long after my neighbor on the opposite balcony had extinguished his lights and retired.

I was tired. The day had been long, the night emotionally exhausting. I was even too tired to get up and go downstairs to bed. It was nicer here. It was cool and beautiful. I would get up and go downstairs later. Downstairs . . . wasn't that a crazy place for a bedroom to be?

I must have slept.

Normally, at whatever hour it actually was, I would have been safely in bed in the bedroom wing, insulated from unusual sounds by a long corridor and several closed doors. All the lights in the villa were out. Presumably L'Oasis slept.

Normally, far away in my bedchamber, I would have heard nothing. But I was not in my bedchamber. And so I heard it: just the smallest of sounds, a mere whisper of something being moved or moving or passing. And I was immediately wide-awake.

I did not move.

Then I heard it again — the least distinct of sounds. It came from the library.

Then silence, as if the intruder himself were listening.

I stayed very still, my mind racing.

A passkey to the gate. A passkey to the house. Both easily obtained. Not even needed. Didn't Nicole let her all favorite guests stay here? There could be a dozen legitimate keys in circulation.

And what about cleaning people, painters, workmen?

But I couldn't sit still forever. If I remained silent, I might be stumbled upon at any second, and I did not yearn for a confrontation.

I had one advantage: The intruder obviously expected me to be blissfully asleep in my bed like any normal person at this hour, whatever the hour was.

And there was a second advantage. French people are electronic and gadget maniacs; Nicole and her house were no exceptions.

I slipped off my shoes. In my bare feet, trembling with awareness of danger, I moved silently off the balcony and into the drawing room until I reached the fireplace. There I picked up a poker. Then I reached over to the adjacent cabinet and pressed a button, twisted a dial.

A stereo system blared out at full volume in every room of the house. Earsplitting is not an adequate description of the effect.

After a pause of several seconds, while I mentally counted the number of steps on the stairway I hoped the intruder was now rapidly descending, I pushed another button. Every light in the house blazed on at once. If the entire world wasn't now awake and wondering what was going on at L'Oasis, it was no fault of mine.

With a death grip on the poker I marched downstairs. A check of the front garden revealed an open gate and the barely visible shape of a disappearing car. It was too dark to make out a license or anything else that might have identified the automobile.

I went back inside and shut off the stereo, noting that lights had sprung on in the villas and apartments around me. Apologizing mentally to them all, I returned to the library to see what, if anything, had been stolen.

The room was in a bit of a mess. The intruder's interest seemed to have been concentrated on the bookcase, for there were books all over the floor. Otherwise, there was no obvious damage.

Odd, I thought – a literary thief. I'd glanced at those books when I first arrived. The usual fare. Novels. Best sellers. Magazines of no intellectual importance. Certainly nothing worth stealing. Puzzling.

And beyond the disorder of the library, nothing appeared to be disturbed. Well, I would clear up the mess in the morning.

I shut the gate and propped a garden chair in front of it. I shut the door and dragged a heavy foyer cabinet in front of it.

I went to bed. In the bedroom this time.

And I slept. I can't believe it, but I did.

Chapter 16

As it turned out, nobody went to Moustiers the next day. Nicole called at seven forty-five to alert me to the fact that all plans were off. "It's going to be a day of killer heat," she said. "Definitely not a day to be traveling. The only way to survive is to come for lunch and spend the afternoon in my pool."

The arrangement suited me well enough, especially as I had not worked out in my mind how it would be possible simultaneously to be traveling to Moustiers in search of pottery and also be painting the mayor of Nice. She didn't mention last night's nocturnal visitor. She must have slept through the commotion. I didn't mention him either. There would be time to tell her later, when I saw them all at lunch. But I did discuss the visitation with the mayor during our morning session.

"Whatever he had in mind, I must have startled him out of it," I told him.

It was almost too hot to paint, and because of the heat, Albert had lowered the blinds in the breakfast room, which changed the quality of the light. It was disconcerting. Ribot's features took on a whole new look I couldn't quite define.

He reached out to hold my hand, wincing slightly. "The board, I'm sure. You must be careful."

"It couldn't be the board. They're the ones who brought me down here. Why would they then send someone to . . ." But I couldn't think of an ending for the sentence. To what? To move books around?

"I'm getting better every day. I can take proper care of you as soon as I'm back on the job. I'd like to get you out of that villa — move you in here, for instance, see that you're safe." He definitely looked better. There was a dynamism about his person, a faint vibration of coiled springs waiting to be released that promised his full recovery. His hand was warm, strong.

"Now," he went on, "about this night visitor; I'm not suggesting it's the entire board; what I'm saying is that it is probably a single member. My would-be assassin. A spoiler. Was anything stolen?"

I hadn't done a real inventory, but everything except the books had appeared to be in order. "I don't think so. Just some books messed up. I'll look more carefully later when I put them away."

"Could it have been you he was after?" In the dim light his expression was somber.

"I doubt it. He'd have headed for the bedroom if that were the case."

"Maybe the visit was to ascertain if you were in touch with me, if there were any clues to my whereabouts, to when I'd return. Any letters. Any communiqués. There will no doubt be another attempt on my life. But this time I'll be ready. And you, my dear Mrs. Willum, had better protect your pretty self by having your burglar alarm fixed pronto."

"I intend to," I assured him.

The rest of the painting session passed in silence, each of us lost in our own thoughts. I was glad when it was over. The light was rotten, the heat was stifling, and I was in a foul mood. I knew why, too: It was because I was getting suspicious of everybody. Imagining the unimaginable. Composing the worst scenario. Slowly but surely turning against the people who had befriended me.

I didn't like myself for it.

But neither did I like myself for not being candid with Ribot, a man who had already survived one attempt on his life and confidently expected another.

Chapter 17

"The only possible thing to do on a day like this," Nicole de Plessis said, meaning a day without even a hint of a breeze, "is exactly what we're doing."

What we were doing was splashing in and out of Nicole's round Roman-inspired pool with the hand-painted terracotta blue fountain in the center.

"There'll be a breeze by four." Julie Savage was a tall, bronzed column of flawless flesh wrapped in a scrap of black-and-white diamond-patterned material so scant there was room for only two diamonds. "Maybe even sooner. You'll see." She plunged into the water, spraying us all as she hit the surface in a racing dive. Strong, slashing strokes pulled her back and forth across the pool, her wet brown arms flashing in the sunshine.

Most of us were there, summoned by the same early-morning call I had received. "It's going to be frightful today, an inferno. Come for lunch when the cannon goes off at the

Château, and bring a bathing suit."

Everyone in Nice set his clock by the cannon's boom at noon. Legend was that a wealthy Englishman had begun the tradition of shooting it off in order to summon his wife home from the beach for lunch. At its sound all commerce stopped dead. Shop doors closed, and the streets filled with a mad rush of traffic homeward bound for the sacred, two-hour lunch.

We never could have gone to Moustiers. It was too hot, just as Nicole had predicted.

So the cannon had sounded. Its wispy thread of smoke had duly ascended into the azure sky. The smell of cooking had also ascended into the azure sky and now hung over the city like a fragrant mushroom cloud composed of real mushrooms.

At Toujours Gaie a luncheon buffet was laid out on a long table under a French blue awning and presided over by a very superior houseman and a small black-haired Spanish maid. I was working on a salad and a pastis between laps in the pool. My pastis was mostly water. Jim Mustard, almost bursting out of a shockingly brief pair of bathing trunks and not the least self-conscious about it, was bending over Robin Wilson, who was dressed mostly in a single green string with other small strings across vital places. B. B. Benezit had gone off with

Longhi and the Clough-Whites on Franck's yacht. Her absence had emboldened Mustard to the point of indecency; he was applying suntan lotion to Wilson's back in strokes that were long, loving, and frankly lascivious.

Wilson, gleaming with a galaxy of gold chains, watches, and bracelets, was stretched out beside the princess, face down on a blue lounge. The princess seemed to be asleep. Perhaps it was for the best, considering the performance that was going on beside her. I was frankly embarrassed, but it didn't seem to bother anyone else; the affair was old news to this group.

If, however, the princess was really asleep, she was doing a miraculous job of not spilling the tall iced drink of unknown composition clutched fiercely in her right claw. She was wearing one of her usual neck-to-toe silk dresses, and a large straw hat had been added to the ensemble to protect her balding head from the sun.

Nicole was also in a straw hat, this one big enough to shield us all from the sun. The rest of her was decorated with two morsels of cotton, and that was it, except for silver hoops dangling from her ears and a regiment of matching hoops marching up either arm.

Guarnieri, in a white embroidered shirt over

navy trunks, was bustling about being nice to everyone.

"The others have gone to Monaco on Franck's yacht," he explained to me.

"Gamblink?" A voice like echoes of an Alpine storm rattled out from beneath the smaller of the straw hats. "How can de Clough-Whites afford to gamble? Dey are dirt poor."

It occurred to me that the princess might know a lot about the pitfalls of gambling; the Russian and other assorted royalty that had constructed its "palaces" in the hills of Nice had been addicted to it. Gambling had ruined many of them. It also occurred to me that the Clough-Whites were never described as anything but "dirt poor," poor things.

"They've just gone to Monaco sightseeing for the day," Nicole told her. "Clough-White has been off his feed for several days, his wife says, and she thought the trip would cheer him up."

"Off his feed . . . that one?" They all laughed. "He never stops eating, eats enough for all of us."

But Nicole was serious. "No, truly . . . don't laugh. She says his computer has broken down, and he's beside himself."

I was missing something somewhere. "His computer?"

Guarnieri took pity on me. "His fabled, infallible memory for faces. The memory the

British used to use before the computer came along."

"Oh, yes . . . I remember."

"So she thought a day on Franck's yacht would do him good, give him a change of pace. Stop him from worrying about his computer failure."

A wicked thought flashed into my mind. I couldn't repress it. Wouldn't an art lover with a computer memory know that Edward Everett Simms was not the name of a sixteenth-century painter? Of course he would. So what had that game been all about?

The princess was still carrying on about the Clough-Whites. "Monaco — dat's gamblink!"

Mustard reached over and patted her, momentarily abandoning his work on Wilson's back. "Maybe they've just gone to watch," he shouted soothingly.

She jumped back from his touch. "I'm not DEAF."

"Sorry." He turned his attention back to Wilson, who now stirred and sat up. He was thin, but well muscled — obviously someone who paid attention to his body. He wasn't the only one; both Nicole and Mustard were watching him appreciatively.

It amused Julie. "He distributes his favors equally," she whispered to me. "He doesn't play favorites." She giggled.

137

"Isn't that a new watch?" someone asked.

"Solid gold." Wilson stretched his arm out indolently to be admired.

"Where did you get it?" Mustard seized the arm and twisted it to have a closer view of the timepiece.

"You're hurting me! I bought it, that's how I got it."

"Where did you get the money? Where do you go nights? You don't have money for a watch like this. Where did you get it?" If I weren't seeing it with my eyes, I would never have believed the scene taking place before me. Mustard was behaving like a jealous husband.

"You think I don't have money, that I have to depend on you for everything? Well, you're wrong. I have resources."

Nicole tried to forestall the impending crisis. "Robin has many friends, I'm sure. People like to give him presents. Nothing wrong with that, is there?"

Mustard wasn't buying. "Loyalty – there's such a thing as gratitude."

"Do my back, Mustard. I need more oil. And stop complaining. You don't own me." Wilson obviously felt in complete control.

"You've got enough grease on you already to swim the English Channel."

"That's not fair. You know how easily I burn."

"I can keep an eye on him now that he's staying in my pool house," Nicole said. "The sun is deadly to a tender skin."

The little maid was rushing around, offering everyone hors d'oeuvres. The princess woke up and accepted a full plate. Her jaws began to work like a threshing machine.

Guarnieri tried politely to draw attention away from her. "Did you read in *Matin* the other day that the stolen paintings had all been returned?"

I didn't know any had been stolen. "What stolen paintings?"

"Something's always being stolen here. We're all quite used to it. Thank God it's never happened to my Bonnard or my Chagall." Nicole stood up, shed her hat, and dived into the pool. When she surfaced again, she swam to where we were sitting and floated on her back at our feet, staring up at us through long, wet lashes. "Although it doesn't matter. The paintings always get returned, sooner or later."

"You have a Chagall?" I'd only seen the Bonnard.

"It's in my bedroom. Bought it ages ago from Chagall himself. Go have a look anytime. It's rather good."

James Gallop Mustard motioned for the houseman to refill his drink. So far he hadn't touched food. He finished the drink in one long swallow and signaled for another.

"It's true," Guarnieri said. "They're always found."

Nicole laughed and did a smart backstroke to the other side of the pool, avoiding the fountain as neatly as if she had eyes in the back of her head. Then she flipped around and returned, fetching up at our feet again. "It's always kept very quiet because these things happen when a collector or museum down here doesn't bother with insurance. What happens is that the thieves negotiate with the owners until a suitable price is arrived at — usually less than what the painting would fetch on the open market."

"The ransom is paid. The painting is returned. Everyone is happy." Wilson sounded nervous. "Mustard, how about some food? You're drinking too much. And bring me something while you're at it."

To my surprise, Mustard stood up and marched docilely to the buffet table. Nicole went thrashing back across the pool, and Guarnieri threw off his shirt and joined her.

Mustard made a show of putting food on his plate. A dab here, a dab there. "A lot of things are kept quiet around here."

"You mean, art thefts?" I was all attention.

He signaled for another drink. "How about murders?"

"Surely not here in Ribot's city?"

The hearing-deficient princess rallied instantly. "Aspretto — dot's not here. Dot's combat swimmink, military goinkson. So a body or two — who cares?"

"One body, to be exact, Princess," Mustard corrected. "And they suspect the job wasn't done there but on the mainland. So a little art theft now and then pales by comparison."

Was he doing a masterful job of trying to change the direction of the conversation? If so, he wasn't in luck.

Julie sat down beside me, her red-gold hair almost blinding in the sun. "Nicole," she said, "won't admit it, but her Chagall *was* stolen. And ransomed back. She doesn't like to talk about it because she doesn't want to admit she doesn't carry insurance and fix her burglar alarm."

"Dot's right." The princess was a perfect example of selective hearing.

Julie continued. "Longhi keeps nagging her to get insurance. He thinks she's crazy. But I don't. None of us bothers with security and insurance; insurance is very expensive. It's cheaper to ransom something back, and burglar alarms are a nuisance."

"Cottage industry," the voice beneath the hat roared.

"What do you think about Longhi?" I asked.

Julie's already big eyes widened another inch.

141

"What should I think? He's presentable. He works hard for our cause, even though this is his first season. He's not really permanent; he's staying in the house of the widow of the old minister of defense, who is very active with us. He's a sort of stand-in while she's away at Fontainebleau, training for some big dressage event. Horses are her mania."

"So you don't know much about him?"

"He couldn't come better recommended. No one questioned *your* credentials. It's not our way." Her normally friendly voice was now distinctly frosty.

"Any friend of Véronique d'Esmé iss a friend of ours," the princess pronounced. "After all, her husband vas minister of defense."

"He's her houseguest," Julie added, as if that concluded matters.

I was beginning to wish I had never broached the subject.

"D'Esmé was under Pompidou, I think," Julie continued. "Very highly regarded."

"Forgive me for bringing it up. I just wondered . . ."

"She couldn't have left a better substitute than Guy. We're all devoted to him."

"Dot's right," the princess thundered. "All da men in Véronique's family vas Cadre Noir at Saumur."

"I see. Very military." I seemed to be losing

142

the thread of the whole conversation, and I flailed about for a way out.

"Who's military?" Guarnieri had emerged from the water and now stood, brown and dripping, before us. He was very fit for a man his age. "Are you talking about Longhi?"

"No. He's not military. He's a geologist. And a handsome one, too." Julie was a one-woman self-appointed defense team for Longhi's case.

"Has got smartz," announced Princess Anna, very firm, very loud.

Julie stepped over to the edge of the pool. "But he doesn't talk very much, does he?" she asked before she dived in.

Nicole now emerged from the water and bundled herself into an enormous towel. "Where were you this morning, Persis? I called you back around ten. No answer. Not out sketching in this heat, I trust?"

First B.B. Benezit wondering, and now Nicole. I prayed that they weren't inspired by more than idle curiosity. Suppose one of them saw me driving off to the mayor's? Suppose they followed?

"I've been trying to thank you for fixing my gate. That was kind of you. Then —"

"Fix your gate?" she interrupted. "I don't know what you're talking about."

She'd probably forgotten. It was a minor detail in her life after all. "The main thing is,

Nicole, that someone came into L'Oasis last night in the middle of the night. Luckily I was able to scare him off. There was no damage done. But I would feel better if the burglar alarm system were fixed. Whoever it was managed to open both the gate and the front door, so —"

"Good Lord!" She was horrified. "But instantly, Persis . . . instantly. So many people have been in and out of L'Oasis over the years . . . so many keys floating around. Have you notified the police — not that they'll do anything. Oh, I'm so sorry. I'll attend to it at once, my dear." She summoned a minion from somewhere and issued rapid orders.

She then dispensed with her towel, crawled underneath her all-enveloping hat, and dropped into the chair beside me to watch Julie race back and forth across the pool. "Young people have such energy." She sighed. "Just look at that child. You wouldn't think she had a problem in the world, would you?"

"What a tragedy about her mother and her breakdown."

"Yes. It's an old scandal. And not a very big one by today's standards. It wouldn't get an inch of press space these days in the trashiest of rags. We don't discuss it. Both Julie and her mother have suffered enough."

For the second time in the same afternoon I

had broached the wrong subject. "I'm sorry."

"No, no. It's quite all right. I understand your sympathy.... Very sensitive of you, Persis. But you must realize that we all are very protective of Julie. We are like her family. Her father is dead. Her mother . . . well, none of us has seen her in years. Julie wants it that way. She wants us to remember the glorious Victoria Savage, film star. Not Victoria as she apparently is today. Now, my dear," she concluded briskly, ending the subject with great firmness, "I want you to be sure to telephone me when you get home. They should have your alarm working by then. I've sent my own men."

"You're too good to me. I never did thank you for having the villa repainted before I arrived."

She looked vague. "Did I? I'm not usually so extravagant about my properties. I am famous for being very tight with my money."

"Dot vill be da day," mumbled the ancient royal remnant, who, like a superior antenna, appeared to have the gift of gleaning all sorts of odds and ends that drifted by in the air. "Vot presents she giffs . . . vot gifts."

I wondered if she was referring to Wilson's newest gold ornament.

Guarnieri, Mustard, and Wilson, who had been busying themselves at either the buffet or the bar, now rejoined us.

"Have you read *Matin* today?" Mustard picked up the newspaper from a nearby chair and thumped the front page. "Look at this. The French are crazy people. They don't clamp down on terrorism no matter how many people are killed because they have business dealings with the countries that sponsor it — everybody knows that there are 'wanteds' hiding out all over the place — and then they sponsor a world 'summit' conference on antiterrorism right here in Nice. It's all in the paper."

Nicole waved her arm casually, and a dozen silver bracelets slid up and down, ringing out like musical chimes. "Who cares about that dreary stuff? It's extremely boring. . . . Terrorists are boring. There's nothing worse than the boring news. We have more important things to think about. For instance, I have planned a sensational evening for us. It's a secret. And I think we all should go home and rest until dinner."

After the drinks and swimming and lunch we all were half asleep already. Furthermore, Julie's promised breeze had not materialized, and we longed to get out of the sun.

So we left willingly, dreaming of the sensational evening to come.

But on the way I paid a quick visit to the Chagall in Nicole's bedroom. And was sorry I did. When I got home and lay down to rest, I couldn't close my eyes. All I could do was stare at visions of Nicole's Chagall dancing on the ceiling.

Julie said it had been stolen and ransomed back, and Nicole seemed to be quite content with the transaction.

But the Chagall in her bedroom was a fake. I knew it at once.

Had Nicole ransomed back a copy of the original — not too bad, but still a copy?

Did Nicole know?

And what about B. B. Benezit, art critic of renown? Benezit was an expert, at one time considered the best in her field. One look at the painting in Nicole's bedroom, and she, too, would have known it was a fake.

Then why hadn't she told Nicole?

Chapter 18

Nicole had promised a sensational evening, and she delivered it.

First we dined under white umbrellas on the terrace of the Westminster Hotel. At ten, when darkness had fully fallen, we adjourned to the garden at the Esplanade du Paillon, where the American Sixth Fleet Band was presenting a concert of jazz and dancing in the stone forum of the Place Masséna. *"Concert et grand bal gratuit avec le 'Show' band de la VIer Flotte U.S.,"* the announcements had read. Before we were anywhere near the arena the rich notes of Gershwin's *Rhapsody in Blue* floated over the amplifying system, making us tap our feet and hurry forward.

There were ten of them — ten gobs in spanking white sailor suits with black neckerchiefs. Three trumpets. Three saxophones. Drums. Guitar. Bass and piano. Two alternating vocalists, one black and one white. And an orchestra leader who leaped into the air, arms waving, at the conclusion of every number. He said, "Merci," after each set, and the crowd loved it, American accent and all.

People were already dancing when we arrived: gliding, twirling, swooping, cheek against cheek. Nobody loves American jazz more than the French. Unless you count me.

The band was warmed up and swinging, weaving its elegant way through Count Basie, Glenn Miller, and Duke Ellington. Then everyone was jitterbugging, as frenetic as any GI who'd ever jived his way through World War Two.

"Dance?" It was Guarnieri.

"With pleasure."

We set sail with enthusiasm. Predictably he was very good. There wasn't a step he didn't know. Hundreds of lessons, I guessed. Suffered through to charm all the rich widows he'd married.

Longhi was next. Longhi was an athlete with a perfectly toned body, and his dancing was impeccable. Restrained but impeccable. The contrast between the two men was interesting: Guarnieri held me like a dear friend, Longhi like a potential adversary.

The Monaco group had returned in time to join us, and once B. B. Benezit was on the scene, her all-seeing eyes glittering behind enormous dark glasses, the flame between Mustard and Robin Wilson guttered and went out. They minded their manners and did their duty by the ladies on the floor. Wilson surprised me; his dancing was tentative, clumsy, not at all what one would expect of a professional. Mustard, on the other hand, seized me firmly by the waist and sallied forth as if we were leading a cavalry charge: Any obstacle was simply run over and dispersed.

Clough-White and Franck didn't dance. It was doubtless a mercy. Probably neither of them had the talent for it.

Everyone was having a marvelous time. Before long perfect strangers were cutting in. Nicole, Julie, B. B., and I whirled from partner to partner, scarcely finishing five steps with any one person. Even dowdy Elizabeth Clough-White joined the fray. The princess — less fragile than one would think — sat on the stark stone steps of the forum without complaint; Nicole had brought a cushion for her. A big red moon sailed giddily over our heads.

I played a game with myself. If I were to judge a man's character by his dancing, what would I conclude? Easy. Wilson was an egoist. Mustard, a bully. Guarnieri, a gentleman. And Longhi? Longhi was a question mark.

Wilson was dancing by himself now, passionately — like a woman advertising her body. Every time he came out on the floor alone the other dancers made a place for him and looked embarrassed.

Mario snatched me from a stranger's arms to lead me through some impossibly complex and elegant tango steps. At the conclusion we finished in perfect harmony. I couldn't believe it.

Then I was back with Mustard, a painful contrast.

"Guarnieri's a wonderful dancer," I said, not too tactfully, as we plowed our relentless way across the floor. "Like the violin of the same name – smoothly perfect."

"His name's not Guarnieri," Mustard said crossly, bulldozing somebody aside so he could keep an eye on Wilson.

"Oh?" So I wasn't the only one who knew. *Nom de sport.*

"You mean a professional name, like a Hollywood actor?"

"Exactly." He elbowed some unfortunate, tramped on a few feet, and we continued our pursuit of his beloved.

"Racing's a glamorous business here; you need a glamorous name. Real name couldn't be commoner – Grappi or something like that. I forget exactly what."

I saw B. B. Benezit standing on the edge of the crowd. She was flirting with a perfectly strange man.

"Who's she picked up?" Mustard wondered, not really interested.

151

The stranger turned away, and B. B. stepped out on the floor with Longhi.

"Where's Robin?" Mustard turned in all directions. "Where has the little bastard got to now? I'd better find him." And without any excuses, he abandoned me where we stood. It didn't matter; somebody came to the rescue at once.

I began to wonder if I was dancing holes in the soles of my shoes; it wouldn't be the first time. The black vocalist had the mike now. He was crooning: "graduation's almost here, my love . . . teach me tonight. . . ." I'd lost track of most of our group.

Suddenly Elizabeth Clough-White was out on the dance floor alone, tugging at me. "Robin Wilson's disappeared. We have to find him. Jim Mustard is frantic."

"He must be around here someplace. I saw him talking with Franck not long ago."

"No, no . . . Mustard says he never goes off like this."

But Mustard knew better. What had he said during the discussion about Robin's new watch? "Where do you go nights?"

B. B. Benezit was standing beside us, quite unruffled. "Why all the fuss? He'll turn up. He always does."

She was right, as it turned out.

We circulated through the crowd without

finding Wilson. Then we moved beyond the area of the lighted arena.

As B. B. Benezit had foreseen, he turned up almost at once. He hadn't gone a hundred feet. He was right there, out of the light, face down like some of the young people lying around listening to the music. It was Elizabeth Clough-White who stumbled over him. And when she bent down and shook him and turned him over, she gave a scream that stopped the Sixth Fleet Show Band in mid-note.

Robin Wilson had been neatly and effectively garroted. For the first and probably the only time in his life he did not look pretty.

Nicole de Plessis, ever the executive, took charge at once. "Someone call the police. Guy — where's Guy? And Mustard, for heaven's sake, do something about the way Robin looks — it's revolting."

But Mustard couldn't. He had rushed away from us and was doubled over, being ill in the street. He was still being ill when the police arrived.

Chapter 19

For the next two days the talk was of nothing but Robin Wilson. His shade was with us every minute, even after the police had finished their questioning and his body had been shipped back to wherever it came from. Nicole had placed Mustard in charge of the latter detail on the theory that he would handle the arrangements most reverently and – more important – would know to whom and where to mail the remains.

They talked of him constantly. Wilson's beauty (which had been obvious). His wit (which had not). His charm (never revealed to me).

We saw little of Mustard. He was in mourning. Surprisingly even B. B. Benezit was morose when I should have thought she'd be rejoicing. Nicole was frequently in tears. The princess made lugubrious noises. Julie was heard to say that though unquestionably shallow in character, Wilson was not actually malicious. The Clough-Whites assumed the mien of professional mourners. Longhi and Guarnieri walked around looking grave and saying little.

None of them actually seemed to know exactly how to behave in the situation, probably because Wilson had played such an ambiguous role in their lives. He had arrived on the scene from nowhere, picked up in the city of Nice by Mustard under circumstances on which no one seemed able to agree. The official role assigned to him by the group, by common consent, had been that of house pet and entertainer. Extra man. Dance partner. Occasional lover. His function was to be an amusing and decorative addition to their ranks and nothing more. He had fulfilled his role well.

The day after his death they gathered at the Negresco Hôtel's five-star Chantecler restaurant to mourn him. Also to dine, to be bowed to reverently at the entrance by the doorman in his red and blue hunting costume, and to be ministered to personally by Chef Maxima himself.

The board knew how to do everything right — including mourn.

"Robin would appreciate our remembering him this way, poor darling. He loved this place." Nicole, as usual, was leading the parade. The Baccarat crystal chandeliers glittered above her. The gold-leaf-painted columns shimmered.

The priceless tapestries glowed.

She was right; he would have.

"After the violent and unattractive way he died, tonight will help to put things right, erase the image of —"

Benezit interrupted. "The hideous way he looked. God, it was so awful —"

"Stop it!" Julie cried. "It wasn't his fault. He'd want us to remember him the way he was before. . . ."

"Beautiful." Mustard barely spoke above a whisper.

"Yes," said Nicole.

"They wanted his jewelry, obviously. He shouldn't have gone downtown wearing all that solid gold." Clough-White's wife, who didn't own any jewelry, gold or otherwise, got to the heart of the matter.

"It's true. The way things are today, it doesn't pay to wear real jewels in public." Surreptitiously Nicole turned the emerald and diamond ring on her finger so that it didn't show. "Are you wearing your real jewels to the reception at Versailles after the Gainsborough Brown vernissage?"

That set them off on a whole new tack.

"I hear the queen's coming. So probably I will wear everything I own," Julie said.

"The whole world's coming. . . ." Clough-White was obviously thrilled.

The whole world wasn't coming. I wasn't, for example. I'd had my moment in the sun at Deauville. Fair was fair.

"Robin would have loved to be there."

"But he wasn't invited, you know."

"I'd forgotten. Only the board. I guess the administration wants our votes."

"Well, we do have some influence after all."

"Poor Robin. So pretty. So harmless."

"So like a Greek god." Mustard.

"That body. Which reminds me, I'll have to shed *pounds*. What do you think of the California Terrace at Monte Carlo for dieting? The Mirabeau's about two thousand dollars a week." Nicole.

"They say Badgestein's the only place to go. Luckily I don't have a problem." B. B.

"He vasn't importand enough to be killt." The princess, rumbling.

"What?" They didn't know what she was talking about. But I knew. Poor Robin Wilson of the gold jewelry and the priceless watch and the mysterious nights and the catholic sexual preferences. Poor Robin Wilson, who wouldn't be going to Paris with or without his jewelry, with or without an invitation.

And I thought the princess had made a remarkably astute assessment. Poor Robin had not been important enough to be killed. Not even for his jewelry.

"She means Robin," I told them.

"Oh." There was a hush.

"I feel guilty," Nicole said, finally. "It was my idea to go downtown. I'd planned for it to be such a sensational evening."

"Well, it certainly was. But how could you know?" Clough-White consoled her. "He shouldn't have worn all that junk. He shouldn't have wandered off. God knows who he was talking to. He should have stayed with us."

Mustard looked as if he might begin to cry. "He should have stayed —"

"Oud off our lifes." It came, surprisingly and in an offhand, ruminating way, from the relic herself.

A large man dressed mostly in black-rimmed spectacles that magnified his eyes to the size of fried eggs now ambled up to our table and pulled up a chair.

"Greetings, group."

Everyone shook hands, solemnly.

"Great shame about your friend," he said. "Depletes the ranks, doesn't it?"

B. B. Benezit was instantly defensive. "He wasn't board, you know. Just a supporter of our cause, you might say. Persis, this is Jacques Chabrier of Monte Carlo Radio. Persis Willum painted the famous portrait of Gainsborough Brown, and she's here on our behalf to paint Jules Ribot."

"Oh, yes." He seemed to know all about it. "Nicole told me. So you're going to paint the mayor?" He looked me over carefully, his Orwellian eyes politely curious. "Have they warned you yet about the mayor? Did they tell you he eats pretty ladies like you for breakfast? You'd better careful. He's a professional charmer. Women have been known to attempt suicide because of him."

"Jacques, you fool ... you'll scare her to death." Nicole laughed, making light of his remarks. "Ribot wouldn't hurt a fly; he *loves* good-looking ladies. Jacques, you have the latest word on everything. When is Ribot coming back? Persis would like to get started; she can't wait around forever, much as we love having her."

"She does add a nice touch to the scenery, doesn't she? How about lunch tomorrow?"

"Jacques, stop it. He's married, Persis, so tell him no. Seriously, Jacques, what about Ribot? What's the word in your newsroom?"

He sighed. "Well, I can't be blamed for trying. Now, about Ribot, the inside story seems to be that he'll be back for the Bataille de Fleurs."

"I told you!" Nicole was very pleased with herself.

"And the inside story, if you're really interested, is also that there really was an assassination attempt but that his people are trying to cover it up because they are afraid it might affect his chances in the election. People don't want to vote for a president who might be the *late* president next day."

The board all laughed derisively and in unison. Nicole laughed loudest. "You don't know Ribot if you believe that. He's cooked it all up for the publicity. Why can't you find out where he is anyway?"

"There are rumors that he's here, rumors that he's there, but he never is." He stood up and bent over my hand to kiss it. "Remember what I said, Ribot is a dangerous man. Don't let him seduce you. You may never get over it. He's like a fatal disease."

A mental image of the mayor leaped into my mind — and the image was all male, all hard muscle, all flashing good looks.

"There are probably," I said, "worse ways to go."

"Amen to that," said Nicole. "There definitely are."

And thus ended the evening.

Chapter 20

Jules Ribot had little to say about Robin Wilson's death.

He knew about it, naturally; he knew about everything that went on in his city. He knew I'd been present. He said he was devastated that I should have had such a terrible experience. He said he hadn't known Wilson personally. He wondered if a member of the board could have done him in.

"I told you they're bad news, my dear."

"Impossible. We all were right there together. He wandered off. He was wearing tons of gold jewelry. It was robbery."

Ribot's dark eyes burned into mine. He had a way of looking that seemed to strip you right down to your socks. I should have hated it, but I didn't; I guess because he made it politely clear that he admired what he saw.

"You are probably right, and I like your loyalty. But I am concerned nonetheless."

"I am perfectly safe," I assured him. "I do not wear real jewels, and I never stray from the crowd. I came here to paint your portrait, and that is what I intend to do. *All* I intend to do."

"I hope not all. When I am better, I should like to show you my city," he said. "Perhaps I could persuade you to stray from the crowd with me . . . just for a while." He was smiling warmly.

"Perhaps."

I buried my nose in my painting and worked furiously. I didn't want him to guess just how easily I could be persuaded. I didn't want to be another one of his conquests, another campaign ribbon on his chest.

There was something absurd about it: I was already fighting a battle to resist him and he hadn't even announced the war.

Chapter 21

There are a million motorcycles and motorbikes in Nice. There must be a minimum of one per inhabitant. Ergo, to select a single one from the buzzing hive that pervades the city would require more expertise than the average citizen could ever possess.

But out in the countryside it is another matter entirely. To begin with, there is rarely another vehicle in sight. Therefore, the motorcycle idling along behind, pausing when I paused, stopping when I stopped, became distinctly noticeable – even to a preoccupied, vague, mildly dreamy artist type like me.

I had set out for Claviers, which is far back in the hills where parachutists had landed during the debarkments. The group, nervous and apprehensive because of the recent death, had drawn into a tight knot of self-protection and was insulating itself with work. This afternoon its members were consulting, en masse, with the "best masons on the Riviera" apropos the reclamation of a particularly decrepit ruin downtown. I'd been invited to participate in the conference with the princes of plastering but had begged off; it was too good an opportunity to take off for an afternoon of sketching on my own.

It was a longish trip, especially as I stopped here and there along the way for a quick sketch of anything that intrigued me. But presently I found myself and my car climbing the hill to Claviers, which was perched like a lookout on the edge of a vast series of valleys, cliffs, and vistas.

I'd been vaguely aware of the motorcycle that dogged me, but only vaguely, because to see such a vehicle in France is as ordinary as seeing one's own arms and legs – it's just always there.

The only difference was that this one didn't pass. French motorcycles always pass; it's the macho thing to do. Tornadoes of smoke and fumes and noise and pebbles; then – whoosh – they're by and out of sight around the next corner while you're still trying to steady your nerves and hang on to your hat and keep your car on the road.

But not this one.

I thought of the episode at the market at the top of the hill near Mount Boron. I thought of the man in the black bubble helmet, the man I'd thought might be Longhi's chauffeur, the man on the rue de la Liberté, or even my neighbor. Then I chastised myself for being over-imaginative.

It was only a motorcycle after all. Just because Wilson had been killed was no reason to think everyone was menacing me. The motorcycle at the market had been nothing — my lurid imagination, as usual. And this rider behind me looked like every other cyclist on the road: leather jacket; boots; black bubble helmet. He wouldn't pass me, it's true. But maybe he wasn't in a hurry, wasn't suicide-minded like the rest of the French one encountered on the road.

I eased my car into the Claviers town square and parked. It wasn't a very big square, even by perched-village standards. There was a restaurant-café, a post office, a church, and nothing more. But I had seen enough on the way up to the town to realize that the views would be spectacular, and I wasted no time getting my sketching materials together and exploring the up-and-down streets until I found a view I liked. There I settled down and promptly lost myself in my work.

When the shadows grew long, I realized it must be late afternoon and time to start for home; so I packed up my things and walked back to the café, where there were tables strewn carelessly around in the square. One or two villagers lazed in the metal chairs, nursing coffees or *citrons.*

"Lemonade," I said to the middle-aged waiter who finally came to take my order.

"He has gone inside," he said.

I thought I hadn't heard correctly.

He leaned over, keeping his voice low. "Back here in the hills, madame, we do not like the law. We stay together, protect each other. I will pretend to get your drink, madame, but when I go inside, you must leave quickly."

"What do you mean?"

"He has been watching you. I lured him inside for a whiskey on the house. I don't know what you've done, madame, but go. If it is an affair of your husband – a lover . . . we know the type well – there is no mistaking it. He is either the law or a criminal. To us there is little difference. Do you know that back here in the hills the police – our own police – were worse in the war than the Germans? Oh, yes. Go now. We don't want types like that in our village, so go, and go quickly."

I looked inside the restaurant. There was indeed a man at the bar. His back was to me. In spite of the heat, he still wore his jacket, as if to take it off would deprive him of both his manhood and his authority. There was a plastic helmet on the stool beside him.

He turned his head, not looking at me, not

yet aware of my presence.

I saw that whoever it was, it was not Longhi's chauffeur. Longhi's chauffeur was clean-cut. Could it be the one who had accosted me on the rue de la Liberté? Who?

I slipped out of my seat, crossed the square, got into my car, and released the brake. Without a sound the Ford slid down the hill from Claviers. Once around the corner, I put it in gear and let the Cortina do its stuff. I didn't dare return the way I'd come; that would have been too easy. Instead, I took every twisting back road that came my way, certain the motorcycle would gamble on my having retraced my original route.

"Never do the expected," Ed Simms had once counseled me.

So I didn't. I never saw the motorcycle again. At least, I don't think so. The truth of the matter is that once back in Nice, I wouldn't have recognized it anyway — or the driver, for that matter.

Nevertheless, from that time on I began to feel that there were two of me wherever I went: me and my shadow. But I couldn't prove it.

Chapter 22

The next day Anton Franck's yacht blew up, and Anton Franck and his steward blew up with it.

There was some question among the police whether or not it had been an accident. There was even a question whether or not the bits and pieces they found were those of Franck and his steward. Both were unaccounted for.

Thereafter our time was spent with the police in the persons of Inspectors Christian Laroux and Roger L'effarque. The princess was dismissed almost immediately on the grounds of age and their inability to conceive of her having planted a bomb or even having portaged one. The rest of us were severely, if courteously, grilled. In deference to the social stature of the board, we had been asked to make ourselves available at Nicole's villa rather than downtown, and we did.

The inspectors spent hours interviewing us one at a time and several times over in Nicole's library, while the non-interviewees waited on the terrace or in the drawing room under the impersonal gaze of a gendarme. Laroux and L'effarque rushed in and out all day, answering phone calls, receiving important bulletins, and generally carrying on like leads in a good French *flic* film. Both were under forty, bronzed, and frighteningly handsome. This last attribute made the grilling easier for the women to endure, although one couldn't be sure about Elizabeth Clough-White, who might have been beyond such considerations.

I had the impression that the two inspectors weren't terribly interested in me, at least as a potential bomber. In my case their questions centered on how Franck had behaved when I was aboard his yacht for dinner, if he was nervous, what was his mood, if there had been any smell of fuel oil, how the servants had behaved. To my surprise I found that they already knew all about me. Like Jules Ribot, they had checked with Interpol. Ed Simms again.

They seemed particularly interested in whether or not I had noted the smell of diesel oil the night I was aboard. I hadn't. All I had smelled was Esteé. The smell of Esteé didn't interest them at all.

I mentioned this to Guy as we sat near the pool, killing time, hanging around and drinking Perrier until or if we were needed.

"Suppose it turns out not to be an accident. Wouldn't we all be suspects, especially after Wilson's death?"

Longhi crossed one elegant white-trousered leg over the other and brushed at an imaginary spot on his white loafer. "Not if the victim is Franck."

"Why not?"

"Well, to begin with, it probably was an accident. It will take days of examining the evidence before they can decide what happened. At this moment the odds are that it was; one has them now and then with these big diesel yachts. Carelessness on someone's part or a faulty engine, a broken fuel line — it can happen."

"I'm glad it didn't happen while I was aboard the *Miranda*. But I didn't smell any fuel oil that night, did you? Not with that perfume pumping through every duct."

Longhi raised a weary eyebrow. "Aphrodisiac. He was into stuff like that. Not the kind of fellow you should have been having dinner with."

I let that go. "But the police don't seem very concerned about the possibility of murder."

"Because they don't care." Longhi smiled wearily.

"Don't care?" Incredible.

"Not in the way you think." He sighed. It was

time for kindergarten class. "Let me explain something to you, my dear. In Nice you have the presence of several hundreds of persons who operate on a petty scale, their fingers stuck in here and there to make a shady buck where they can. The Niçois call them by the Neapolitan name Camorra. They are what you would call petty criminals, hoods. Jules Ribot has disposed of most of them, cleaned them out of Nice. Understand?"

"Yes." I already knew that.

"But there is something else in Nice. There is the presence of the Grand, the real, the true Sicilian Mafia. They had taken over the casinos when Ribot came into office — corrupted legitimate businesses, invaded tourism, were running prostitution, warring over control of the drug traffic. Ribot got them on the run; most now operate out of Marseilles."

I was beginning to have an idea of what was coming next. Franck, the dark, the squat, the simian. "And?"

"And there were chieftains who preferred it here. Chieftains who had 'retired,' who wanted to lead the life of the decent, respected citizen. Who loved the luxury and chic of Mount Boron with its view of Nice and the Riviera."

"You're saying?" But I knew what he was saying.

"That the police suspect, probably know,

that Anton Franck was Grand Mafia. They will shed no tears over his demise."

"I thought he was Greek?"

"He was Sicilian from head to toe. Anyone with money can buy false papers on the Côte d'Azur. A new identity is easier to obtain than a new wife. Anton Franck isn't even a Greek name. Try Antonio Franconi — a real Mafia chieftain or pope. I tried to give you a clue the other night to warn you off. Franconi is well known to the police on the Riviera. He once had many business interests here ... some legitimate, some not; the legitimate served as cover for the illegitimate. It is the way things are done."

I was having a peculiar reaction to the news that I had lately been alone with a now permanently retired Mafia chieftain on his yacht. I had begun to shake like a tambourine. I could hear my knees clanking under my skirt.

Longhi was watching me with an air of amusement. "On the Côte d'Azur you will find everything," he reminded me. "That is part of the charm — and the danger."

"You are a cynic," I told him, still quaking, but less violently. "This place is supposed to be paradise."

"And in paradise," he reminded me, "there was a serpent."

I sighed. "And death. First poor Robin. Now

Franck. And within two days. Could there be a connection? Was Robin really killed for his necklaces? Did Franck's yacht really blow up by accident?"

"The necklaces were missing. We didn't notice at the time; we were too upset. But the police assure us that they were. As for Franck, we shall have to wait for the investigation."

"How did you know about Franck?"

"Everybody knew. He was retired. Détente reigned."

He leaned back and lit one of his black cigars, and we smiled at each other, sitting quietly without further need to talk.

At that exact moment I couldn't have carried on a conversation if my life had depended on it. The yacht ... Franck ... the Mafia ... Nice ... What kinds of people was I involved with here? What was happening to my quiet, sun-drenched painting vacation on the Côte d'Azur?

James Gallop Mustard broke the spell. He stumbled out of the villa and dropped like a fallen cement mixer into a chair. He was breathing hard, the veins on his forehead and neck standing out like ropes. His face had a purplish tinge. I thought he was having a stroke.

"Oh, Jesus," he gasped.

I'd never seen anyone look quite like that.

Certainly he was going to topple over at our feet and die.

"Asking," he gasped, "asking . . ."

Longhi had already jumped up and was getting him out of the chair and flat on the ground. "Wring out one of those napkins in the water. Here, put it here . . . Brandy. In the house — quickly!"

I think he was giving the fallen man artificial respiration, but I'm not sure. I ran, terrified, certain that by the time I returned Mustard, like Wilson and Franck, would have expired.

But I was wrong. When I returned, Mustard was back in the chair and his color was better. He was still breathing heavily, but it was obvious that he was going to stay with us.

"Have these little attacks. Now and then. Mustn't get upset. Sorry." He reached for the brandy.

"Small sips," Longhi ordered. "That's right. It doesn't pay to get worked up about things. Ought to watch your blood pressure, you know. Go on a diet. Ease up on the drinking."

"Perfectly fit. Just a bad turn." Mustard was taking larger and larger sips. His color was back to normal. "Thanks just the same."

Longhi returned to his Perrier. "See a doctor. Wouldn't hurt."

Mustard had drained the last drop of brandy. "Not necessary. Got annoyed with all the damn questioning, that's all. Incidentally, I'd appreciate it if you wouldn't mention this to anyone."

"Promise," we both said, sorry for him.

"Bastards were giving B. B. a grilling. Imagine! Afraid I shot off my mouth, but it made me mad." He tipped the glass on end, searching for a last drop of brandy. Finding none, he heaved himself up from the chair and lumbered slowly back inside the house, like a man returning to the chambers of the Inquisition. I watched his recovery and exit with astonishment.

"What do you suppose all that was about? I thought he was going to die right in front of us. It was a quick recovery."

"Too preserved in alcohol to die."

"There's so much happening."

Longhi smiled, finally. "When in Nice," he told me, "you must expect to find a salade niçoise on your plate — if not for every meal, then at least now and then."

A salade niçoise. Well, that was one way of putting it.

But to me it was more like a pot au feu, a stew cooking on a *very* hot fire.

Chapter 23

By the time the two inspectors finally dismissed us after a day and a half of questioning and an admonition not to leave town without informing them (Nicole informed them immediately that the board members all were going to Paris shortly for the "do" at Versailles, and that was that), we were thoroughly depressed and demoralized.

Two people dead within three days – three, counting Franck's steward . . . unbelievable. The group was dazed.

"And I haven't even mentioned to them that someone tried to break into your house. No use really, as there's probably no connection," Nicole whispered to me.

"Probably no connection between the deaths of Robin and Franck either," I whispered back, hoping it was true.

It was noon by the time the law had finished with us, and we all were drooping about.

"Not that I personally will miss Franck," B. B. Benezit confessed. "He's no great loss to us, except financially. But it's the idea of the thing. First Robin dead, now Franck. It makes me nervous."

"Coincidence, of course. Long arm of, and all that." Clough-White didn't particularly look as if he believed it.

"Dere are alvays trees," the princess — ever the voice of doom — pronounced with satisfaction.

"We can't sit around being depressed like this. The sea will mend us," said Julie. "The sun and the sea cure everything — even the worst. I know. The sun and the sea will cleanse us of the ghosts of Wilson and Franck."

It seemed as reasonable a remedy as any, so we all trooped off to one of the restaurants along the beach, although under the circumstances nobody could stand the thought of food.

Julie had selected the Beau Rivage opposite the defunct hotel of the same name. "It's the best location," she explained. "And quieter than the Lido Plage or the Ruhl or any of the others."

No one disagreed. We all felt the need for quiet.

The sun was warm, but there was a cool breeze from the sea. I was sitting facing the promenade, having decided to avail myself of the moment to improve the tan on my back.

Behind me the *cailloux* rattled and clanked in the gentle waves. The only other people at the restaurant were a family of six, clad in Roman-type plastic sandals like mine, minuscule bathing trunks or G-strings, and absolutely nothing else. Actually the smallest children were clad in nothing at all. I couldn't look in the direction of the grandmother; I found her near nudity unnerving.

"Don't be so American," B. B. Benezit admonished me. "You must understand that to a Frenchwoman of a certain age bosoms are medals of honor; they have done good work and been much admired in a lifetime."

"The fact of the matter is," Guarnieri added comfortingly, "that she probably has a young lover at this very moment."

Everyone was trying very hard to be cheerful, to talk of everything but the subject that preoccupied us all.

I looked the grandmother firmly in the eye and smiled. She smiled back and raised her glass to us. "The French are a curious race," I said for perhaps the millionth time in my life.

Everyone agreed at once, happy to have been presented with a subject that could be reasonably discussed.

"They're certainly very tough in business," said Mustard, who'd said very little about anything since the recent deaths.

"Sell their best friend for a hundred francs." Naturally Elizabeth Clough-White, being ardently British, was equally ardently anti-French.

Her husband broke in quickly; he was a little more Christian. "I wouldn't go quite that far, my dear. But there is certainly this to be said. With all their carrying on about honor and martyrs to the country, and with all their war monuments to the dead, it's a well-known fact that most of the French collaborated with the Germans as soon as they realized the damned Germans had beaten them."

Not surprisingly there was an outcry of protest. Not a raucous one, because oddly enough, the French occasionally enjoy criticizing themselves as fiercely as they criticize everyone else and also because they were happy to be discussing something other than Wilson and Franck.

"One bad apple doesn't mean the whole lot are rotten," Guarnieri offered. "There were plenty of French heroes."

"True." Benezit again. She seemed to have more than a fair grasp of French mores and history. "Look what happened right here. When the Allies landed farther up the coast, the underground rose in Nice to fight the Germans and were slaughtered for their trouble; the Allies didn't turn up until days later. Still, I'm not sure I'd trust a Frenchman with a wooden nickel, let alone my life, much as I love them all."

"Your life may be the one thing you *can* trust him with," Guarnieri insisted wryly. "You must realize . . ."

They drifted into the politest of arguments — Benezit, Mustard, the Clough-Whites (who thought in unison), and Julie on one side; Nicole, Guarnieri, and the princess on the other. Longhi, as always, did not commit himself.

Ordinarily I would have leaped to the defense of the French, but I was too preoccupied. I sat silent, with my back to the sea, watching the people on the promenade while the conversation rattled on around me.

In their colorful bathing clothes, the group reminded me of rotating forms in a kaleidoscope: bright symmetrical silhouettes, changing and hesitating and changing again.

Now one was talking. Now another. One left. Another returned. The cast kept exchanging roles. And as they shifted and changed, the conversation shifted and changed with them while I listened and dreamed.

Julie detached herself from the group and stepped boldly into the water, and I heard them talking about her mother when she was gone. "Poor, poor Victoria, she made her last films here in Nice, you know. . . ."

Then Julie returned, and the conversation stopped abruptly. Mario left next, so they talked about him.

"He's a very stubborn man. He never gives up. . . ."

"Just so. Remember how he drove his whole last race in a body brace up to his neck? Impossible, they said. . . ."

"Had the car's cockpit specially fitted out so he could manage it . . . never has given up about his brother . . . all these years."

Nicole got up to join him in the sea, and not showing favoritism, they immediately started on her.

"She ought to marry him . . . he'd be perfect for her. But she'll never marry again."

"Why not? She's not old, and she has plenty of money."

"No need to marry then. Besides, after the affair with Ribot . . ."

There had been no mention of Nicole and Ribot in the mountains of material I'd struggled through. Nor had there been one single photograph of the two together in all the hundreds of photos I'd seen of him with various women. Had it all been edited?

"That was a good twenty years ago, when he was a struggling young lawyer and she was a new, very rich widow. It was through her connections, in fact, that he was able to move into a new circle of influential people. Without her he might still be an unimportant legal hack."

"Did it end badly — their affair?"

"Who knows? It's been said he jilted her, but that could just be gossip. Certainly she bears no grudge; witness this portrait commission. On the other hand, she's never remarried, although she isn't above keeping house pets." An obvious reference to the late Robin Wilson.

Guy Longhi rose and took off his terry robe. He put it over his arm and strolled off down the beach. I couldn't help admiring the spare efficiency of his body.

James Gallop Mustard must have taken exception to the reference to Wilson as "house pet," but as he couldn't remonstrate in front of his wife, he also stood up and stamped off down the beach. Clough-White had long ago deserted us. Either the conversation bored him or he had an overwhelming need for exercise.

The ladies, left alone, immediately fell into their own peculiar brand of "conversation." It centered mostly on clothes and make-up and the impending marriages and divorces of a whole lot of people I did not know or care to know.

The princess, bundled up as always, had fallen asleep. I would have followed suit, except that the scene on the promenade was too lively:

young people whizzing and whirling about on roller skates and skateboards, racking up a dazzling record of near misses and minor collisions; mysterious women from some exotic North African country — could it be Morocco? — their veils flowing in the wind; joggers panting along, rippling muscles sweat-drenched and gleaming; tourists pausing to admire the bathers and the sea. Children capered. Dogs barked. Everyone was delirious with the beauty of this day.

Suddenly I was no longer drowsy but completely attentive.

Mustard was back with us and had returned to the subject of the perfidious French. Actually he was talking about the two boys hanged near the pedestrian mall. "They weren't exactly caught, you know. I've been told they were betrayed by someone, one of their own, who was currying favor with the krauts." Mustard was one of those who still referred to the Germans with World War I-style insults. "Pretty rotten."

But it wasn't Mustard or what he was saying that brought me to attention so fully. It was what I saw on the sidewalk above the wall that separated beach from street and promenade.

My neighbor, the man on the balcony, was standing there, waiting for the light to change so that he could cross on the green amid a large group of people. And next to him was Clough-White. They stood side by side, with their backs to me. I couldn't see them talking, but I knew they were, because when the light changed, the man on the balcony stepped into the street and crossed, but Clough-White did not.

I would never have noticed them in the hurly-burly of the promenade if I hadn't spotted Longhi's chauffeur first and followed his gaze.

He was halfway up the stairs to the street, lounging on the fourth step from the top.

And when Clough-White turned away from the man he had been speaking to, Longhi's chauffeur also turned away and descended the stairs, then strolled casually down the beach and in the opposite direction.

The rest of the afternoon passed somehow.

I turned in the sun. I floated in the transparent teal blue water. I slathered myself with sunscreen and turned in the sun some more. All around I heard the hum of conversation, the rustle of activity. Cries of children; calls of the *pirates de la plage;* shouts of a group playing volleyball farther down the beach; the purr of passing motorlaunches.

It had nothing to do with me. I was in my own world, far removed from what was going on around me.

Who are these people? I was wondering. Can Ribot be right? What am I involved in?

I tried to divorce myself from the moment, the here-and-now, to think clearly about everything that had passed. The group didn't notice my abstraction; it was too preoccupied with its own affairs.

Until I observed the scene with Clough-White, the man on the balcony, and Longhi's chauffeur, I had succeeded in discounting everything that might have been disquieting about the group because that's the way I wanted it. I was on holiday, a paid holiday. The climate was perfect. The people were charming. My villa was sensational. The mayor was an attractive subject ... attractive in other ways, too.

What could possibly be wrong? Why look for trouble?

True, someone had taken a potshot at the mayor, but he wasn't dead. And wasn't it a chance every politician takes when he aspires to high office? True, Wilson had been strangled, but was it any wonder, with the gold jewelry he flaunted so shamelessly? True, Franck's yacht had blown up and no trace of him remained, but no one had yet established that it wasn't an accident. Even Wilson's death could be considered a sort of accident.

For everything that had happened to date, I had found an excuse to dismiss any troubling questions I might have. I didn't *want* to entertain questions that might spoil my idyll. No complications, please.

Yet questions had arisen this very afternoon. Nicole, for instance. Why, in all the boxes of material documenting every instant of Ribot's career, had there been no mention of Nicole?

What about her phony Chagall? What did that mean?

The Clough-Whites — what were they doing with this group anyway? They weren't rich enough. True, she did all the paper work for the society. But why did they pretend to know about art when they didn't?

And Guy Longhi — why did he keep a chauffeur and drive his own two-seater Porsche?

What did the one-time sensation James Gallop Mustard live on?

And apropos books — what about Guarnieri? Nicole had called him an intellectual illiterate. So why would he be writing a book?

And the man who lived across from me — who was he? Why did he know Clough-White, and why was Longhi's chauffeur interested?

Could it be that this was not an idyll after all but a different kind of scene, a bad one?

Then I pulled myself together. What nonsense. Ribot was just a suspicious politician exposed to the dangers all high-profile politicos must endure as part of the nature of their profession. And the society members – they were just what they seemed to be: wealthy dilettantes dabbling in good deeds that were actually based on the selfish motive of preserving their comfortable way of life. Furthermore, it would be only natural for Nicole to edit all reference of her affair with Ribot from the clippings if he had jilted her, as had been suggested. Mustard? No doubt B. B. Benezit supported him. Maybe he'd made some wise investments with the money from his book. Guarnieri? Well, anyone could try to write a book.

No. There was no evil here. Impossible even to think it. This was the Côte d'Azur, runner-up to heaven itself.

I was the luckiest starving artist on the entire Riviera, possibly in the entire world.

And I'd better not forget it.

Chapter 24

There was a small, dark French car waiting at my gate when I returned to the villa. I recognized that car; I'd seen it before. In Normandy, to be exact. I had, in fact, ridden in it — an experience never to be forgotten.

Sitting inside, naturally, was Jean Claude Tendron, Boy Broadcaster, also small and dark.

He leaped out when he saw me and rushed forward. Waves of energy sprang out around him like flames around a drawing of the sun.

"Persis Willum — at last. I thought you were never coming home."

"You're still in one piece, Tendron? I can't believe it after my last ride with you."

"Oh?" He looked baffled for a moment. Then he remembered. "You mean our ride to the Belle Aurore for lunch? That was nothing. You should see me on the Corniches."

I blanched at the thought. "I can imagine."

He laughed. "Forgive me for chortling, I can't help it. You're so *law-abiding*, you Americans."

I wasn't so sure about that, but I didn't argue. "How nice to see you, Tendron. What are you doing here? Are you on assignment? You did say something about coming down, didn't you?"

He waved his arms around wildly. Tendron never made small gestures. It was not his nature, maybe because he himself was already so small. "Business. Always business. An assignment."

I stared at him in admiration. Not for the Boy Broadcaster the unsullied white of the Riviera. Tendron resembled some exotic tropical bird that had strayed across the Mediterranean from North Africa. His shirt flamed with embattled colors -- reds clashing with oranges, greens fighting purples, yellows in a death struggle with blacks. His slacks were bright pink, and his espadrilles were blue. I thought, however, that his face itself looked pale. Maybe it was an illusion created by all that unbridled tonality.

"Aren't you going to offer me something to drink after my long, hot wait?"

"Of course." The gate gave way so suddenly that I nearly fell down. I'd forgotten it was fixed. "They say there will be rain tomorrow. The people at the market promised," I said when I had recovered my balance.

"If it does rain, it will be only a sprinkle.

You'll see. Three drops at most. It wouldn't dare rain. I gave you my word."

"Well, I wouldn't mind. As long as it's only a drop or two."

I settled him on one of the two white sofas in the living room and asked him what he'd like to drink.

The *bon viveur* shook his head. "Nothing."

I was astonished. "Nothing ... but you said —"

He seemed nervous, jumpy. And he *was* pale. I could see it plainly now that we were out of the sun. "I'm supposed to be in Monaco tonight. Don't really have the time ..."

His mind obviously was not on what he was saying, and his eyes darted around the room, looking everywhere except at me. He reminded me of a child with a confession to make. But Tendron — what could he have to confess? Or was he worried about the portrait?

"The mayor's portrait — I haven't started it yet."

"No?" I don't think he heard me. His tiny, neat feet had begun to drum nervously on the white carpet.

I tried again. "Is it true that Ribot will be the top contender for the presidency?"

"Sorry? Oh, yes. Absolutely. The pundits say so. No question." But he spoke abstractedly.

"In that case," I continued, "I suppose I have

you to thank for the opportunity to paint the person who might be the next president of the republic. So I herewith thank you." For some reason it set him off like a Roman candle.

"But that's it — I feel responsible. It was I who persuaded you to undertake this. And if anything happens . . . You, a foreigner. My career. And just when I am going forward full speed, doing brilliantly — yes, brilliantly."

To my horror I saw tears well up in his eyes as he spoke. His face had grown so suffused with emotion that it now matched the orange-reds of his shirt. I rushed to the bar and poured some water.

"Here, drink this. You must calm down." I really didn't expect that the Boy Broadcaster was doing anything more than dramatizing; the French are prone to high drama over the least little thing. It is a trait that I can well appreciate, being inclined to high drama myself.

His color had now changed back to its original pale ivory. I did not know which shade I found the more unsettling.

"It's this business of Franck," he said finally after a series of coughs and small chokings designed to forestall the necessity of speaking.

Filled with a premonition that it would be well to be seated when he finally got around to his reasons for being at L'Oasis, I sat down across from him.

"What about him?"

He seemed to grit his teeth and brace himself. "The political correspondents for Antenne Two have been researching all the front-running candidates, including — naturally — Jules Ribot. With the elections coming up, it's quite normal; in fact, mandatory." He paused and stared over my shoulder at Mount Albon's lower slopes, which were just visible in the distance. "However," he continued, "the death of Anton Franck has, er, you might say 'intensified' matters. Yes, I believe 'intensified' is a good word."

I was astonished. "What does Franck have to do with it?"

His eyes met mine reluctantly. "Did I say that? Who knows?"

"What are you implying?"

He sighed. "In the beginning Ribot was legal counsel for a number of companies that had business interests in England, in France, and later specifically on the Riviera. There was never any proof that Ribot was a partner, although he was definitely an investor. Current investigation has revealed that these same businesses were undoubtedly fronts for laundering money. Shares were owned by suspicious figures known to be connected with the Italian Grand Mafia, despite the fact that everything was so cleverly set up that there was no solid

192

proof. Anton Franck is known by the police to be Antonio Franconi, not a Greek at all but a 'retired' Mafioso with a false passport and a cleverly constructed false identity."

I knew that much. "But Ribot was the enemy of the Mafia, so what has he to do with Franck, or Franconi?"

"True. He took on the Mafia in order to be elected mayor of Nice; it was his chief platform then and his chief claim to fame."

I seemed to be playing devil's advocate. "Suppose he *had* once served as lawyer for a consortium which was later found to have Mafia connections. It was still he who threw them out of Nice."

"True. Absolutely true."

"Well, then?" I couldn't understand why he was in such a state.

"Well, then, it doesn't matter – don't you understand?"

I didn't. It seemed to me that Tendron was on the verge of a nervous breakdown over nothing. Well, next to nothing.

"Look," he said, chewing furiously on his bottom lip, "we've found out that it isn't just Antenne Two that's investigating Ribot. Alleged Mafia connections – even in the past – are so serious for a presidential candidate that the Deuxième Bureau itself is supposed to be on his trail – has been for some time. Now these rumors that he's been shot. My God . . . what have I got you into? It's all my doing. Everybody knows it. I took all the credit. Now I will get all the blame if anything happens to you. The mayor's been shot. Our sources confirm it. Franck has been blown up under, God knows, mysterious circumstances. . . . I tell you, it's all too terrible. I see my whole career blowing up, too . . . vanishing without a trace, if anything should happen to you. You must leave at once. Forget the whole business. Don't begin the portrait. Get out. Go." He finally looked directly at me, and his eyes had a look of black despair.

"Tendron, are you mad? What are you saying?" The reds and oranges of his shirt shimmered in front of me like mirages on the desert. I could hear him speaking, but he sounded very far away.

"Don't you see, Persis . . . if there's been one attempt on Ribot, if Franck is dead, if someone's after the mayor, if you're near him, painting him . . . don't you see the danger to you, just being on the scene? You must leave, get out. . . ."

A man had spoken to me as I stared at words on a wall.

"Maria, move on," he'd said. "Are you crazy, standing here?"

And L'Oasis — somebody had broken in.

"For both our sakes, go, Persis . . . go." I heard Tendron faintly.

He was coming back into focus. "What do you know about the two boys who were hanged on the rue de la Liberté in 1944? Two boys from the Free French?"

"What are you talking about? What about 1944? Hanged? It happened every day back then. Persis, are you listening to me? Pay attention — this is serious."

"I'm listening. Could you find out for me?"

"About what? About that? What has that to do with now? Ribot will be back any day now . . . you must promise. . . ."

He was gritting his teeth in an effort not to shout at me. "I came all the way down here . . . duty . . . if anything happens . . ."

"Nothing will."

"Hanged boys — you're being crazy. Well, I came to warn you, and I did. For both our sakes, please go home."

And Tendron left, his duty done.

I didn't even see him go. I was thinking about the Deuxième Bureau's investigating Ribot. And I was remembering something Ed Simms once told me: "The best cover for an agent is something completely unlikely. The more unlikely his cover, the less likely he is to be suspected."

Chapter 25

I'd almost forgotten in the shock of Tendron's visit that tonight was to be the Bataille de Fleurs, the one Longhi had referred to the day he picked me up at the airport. "This town in summer is like Versailles under Louis the Fourteenth. The whole world will be there, including the mayor, even if they have to shoot him full of drugs and prop him up on sticks." Something like that.

Perhaps he had exaggerated. Maybe the whole world wouldn't actually be there. But Victoria Savage would, and that was enough for me.

"It's really a big parade with about sixteen floats decorated with beautiful girls and tons of flowers. Our group never bothers to go; we've all seen it a million times. But Mother has been much better these last few days. She's on a new, experimental medicine, and it seems to be working. She's calmer, more rational, almost her old self. So I thought I'd take her. She might enjoy the crowds and the lights and the glamour. It will remind her of old times. Would you like to come, too?"

Would I like to meet Victoria Savage, spend an evening in her company? How could Julie even ask?

"Come to the villa first and have a glass of champagne; the parade won't start until after dark. I haven't invited the rest," Julie had explained, "because I don't want them to see Mother as she is now. I want them to remember her as she was when they first knew her: beautiful; successful; a great international star. Also, I confess, I'm never sure when Mother will remember something or someone. Her ups and downs are unpredictable, often frightening. And a face from her past might upset her. It's important that she not be upset."

Julie had been perfectly calm, perfectly normal. There was no indication that she was discussing anything out of the ordinary, but perhaps that was how her mother's illness now seemed to her.

"But what about me?" I'd asked.

"You will be a new face. A new face always gives her pleasure; there are so few I dare trust. You will be kind to her. You will understand. After all, my mother was an artist, too. Artists understand one another."

I pulled up at Les Fées at exactly the appointed 8:00 P.M., all dressed up and wild with anticipation.

It was my first visit to Julie's villa, although Nicole had pointed it out to me earlier. "She doesn't entertain because of her mother. We all know Victoria is in residence, but we don't see her. She never recovered from that first breakdown here in Nice. There is talk of her having to be kept so heavily sedated that she is almost a zombie. Reduce the medication and she is so excitable that . . ." Nicole never finished.

Nor was Victoria in evidence when I arrived.

"It will be a while," Julie told me. "She's dressing."

There was caviar in a crystal bowl and a bottle of Veuve Clicquot cooling in a crystal bucket. Julie opened it expertly and filled our flutes. "I don't keep servants," she explained, "just Mother's old-timers — those who are left. New servants frighten her; she is afraid she's back in the hospital and is filled with panic. They do terrible things in a hospital. I will never let it happen again."

The salon where we were sitting surprised me. Nothing about it suggested the Riviera. The Charles X furniture was covered in a variety of paisley and silk upholstery; a Louis Philippe sofa was done in petit point flowers. The walls were painted a pale apricot; the carpet was Aubusson.

Julie saw me looking. "It's a mixture, isn't it? You see, I've tried to make everything warm and cozy to give Mother a sense of security — all the things she remembers." She waved at the tables covered with books and bric-a-brac, the multicolored pillows and fur throws on the sofas, the flowers everywhere — freesias, roses, gladioli. There were Oriental bowls and china. Small bronze sculptures. Multicolored candles in multistyled candlesticks. Snuffboxes. Silver dishes. Pearl-handled letter openers. Gold clocks. Bits of marble.

And of course, photographs. Photographs everywhere. And all of Victoria Savage.

"There are no mirrors in the house," Julie said. "These are all we have. When she looks at these photographs, she sees herself. It is the *only* way she sees herself."

"Then how does she manage to dress?" I wondered aloud.

"Isabella. Isabella has always been her dresser. Wait, you will see."

I took my champagne and did a tour of the photographs in the room. Julie explained each one as I went. She was, I couldn't help thinking, a true keeper of the flame, dedicated to preserving a fairy tale.

"This was Mother in her first role . . . she was only sixteen . . . look, you can see the baby fat . . . she still had it, like Marlene Dietrich in

200

her first film, remember? And here she is with De Mille, it was he who made her a star, you know. A terrible taskmaster, but still — and here's wicked Errol Flynn. He was the one who inspired her to try for better roles. 'No more sex symbols,' he told her, 'you're better than that.' The studio killed her, of course. Not literally — but still . . . So she came here. It was Bordolini, the Italian director, who convinced her to come. She really believed. . . ."

It was a story told many times over in newspapers and magazines and even, these days, on television whenever there was to be a Victoria Savage Film Festival. Ancient history.

But not, obviously, to her daughter.

"She looked at it as her chance to become an artist, a master of her craft."

Julie poured more champagne, and I watched, fascinated.

From the beginning she had puzzled me. A thin, delicate-featured girl whose beauty was like a print pulled from a "struck" plate, a blurred and diminished copy of the original. I had always wondered why she was like a red-gold shadow in the group's collection of strong personalities. Now, as she conducted this photographic tour of her mother's career in a hushed and worshipful voice, I unraveled her secret: Victoria Savage was her daughter's reason for living.

"This," she was saying, "is a picture of the last great fete she attended. It took place right here in Nice in 1953, organized in her honor. . . . She was a great international star, making a film in the studios here. They were dazzled by her presence. The most beautiful woman ever to grace the Côte d'Azur, the papers said. I wasn't here, of course; I wasn't born until the next year. But everyone came – kings, princes, millionaires. And the parade – look; those are the pictures. They took all her historical De Mille films with all the pageantry – there were fifteen of them – and they did the floats around them. There were bands, and costumes you couldn't believe, and charioteers, and gladiators and real lions. . . ."

I looked at the photographs, a great montage of them in a hand-carved gold-leaf frame mounted on a section of wall above a marble-topped Louis XV commode.

"Mother sat in the reviewing stand in front of the Negresco, exactly where the mayor sits now. The whole parade was for her. She talks of it sometimes. It may have been, in fact, her last really happy memory. The people cheered. They threw flowers in her lap. There was music – bands playing. Dancers. When she remembers, she is happy."

Thinking of it, Julie Savage was happy, too. "That's why," she continued, "I want to take her tonight. This new medication may make it possible for her to enjoy a spectacle like the one years ago that made her happy."

And just then Victoria Savage made her entrance.

I wasn't prepared. Not in any way.

Oh, I know, I'd been looking at the photographs. The aura of Victoria Savage was all around me, everywhere in the room. No doubt it had been planned that way.

Still, I wasn't prepared.

I heard the voice first.

"Good evening. I am sorry to keep you waiting."

I knew that voice. The whole world knew it. The hesitant, husky tones had been imitated a million times by later would-be goddesses in quest of the magic of Savage's irresistible appeal. None had found it, but the quest went on.

I turned. And there she was.

If De Mille himself had orchestrated it, that entrance couldn't have been more impressive. She had descended some unseen staircase and stood now on the bottom step, her maid, Isabella, holding a silver drapery aside.

She was a Roman statue. White marble. Draped in silver cloth. Her red-gold hair, the famous trademark, was swept up and wound with white gardenias. Silver cloth clung sensuously to her breasts and hips. A silver scarf drifted over her arms. Her marble skin glowed. The fabled legs went on forever.

And her face . . .

Dr. Pitanguy, I thought, you'd better come and have a look at this.

They say that retarded children look like children all their lives, that they never grow old. And Victoria Savage — it was the same for her. Suffering, far from marking her, had arrested her exactly at the time it first occurred.

It was 1953. Nothing had changed.

She stood still for a moment, prolonging the entrance. Then she swept into the room. "Champagne, please. Only a drop. We must not be late."

Julie had already filled the flute. I had seen her do it — not with champagne, but with Évian water.

"It is important," Victoria Savage continued, sipping her "champagne" and not seeming to notice that it wasn't, "never to be late. It is disrespectful to one's public."

Isabella had dropped the curtain and was hovering around the star, adjusting this, fussing with that detail of her costume. And now that Savage was close to me, I could fathom some of the secret of the miracle. Layers of chalky powder covered every exposed inch of her, burying whatever flaws there might be in a sea of marble dust. Her blazing hair had been pulled relentlessly and cunningly to heights that also pulled up any flesh of chin and cheeks and eyes that might have given up and yielded to gravity.

The star was a living monument to her dresser's special skills. The miracle wasn't Victoria Savage; it was Isabella.

Julie knew it, too. "Herbs. Medicines — the natural ones. Diet. Regimen. She's the best there is. Victoria will never let her go."

I noticed that Julie never referred to the actress in her presence as Mother. You might have thought Victoria Savage wasn't even aware that she had a daughter.

Now that the living miracle had been produced, the dresser withdrew, smiling, to be replaced by a young, good-looking, well-dressed male.

"Victoria's secretary," Julie said. But I knew he was a male nurse; the slight lift to Julie's eyebrows told me.

"This is to be," her mother was saying, "a very special evening. They have been working on it for months. Planning. Building. The greatest costume designers brought in. The best production. Props and decorations without regard to cost. An extravaganza. The most exciting since the war. Costs running into millions. Kings and princes and the *crème de la crème*. All Europe . . ."

She paused dramatically. Then she looked at each of the three of us in turn and lifted her champagne flute.

"And all," she said, "for me!"

Victoria Savage was lost to reality. Not only did she look as she had in 1953, but she believed that it *was* 1953 and that she was still a great star, the toast of two continents.

And Julie was playing the game.

"That's right, Victoria," she said. "They will be so pleased to see you."

"Oh, yes," I echoed, playing the game, too. "They'll be so pleased to see you."

Because who knows? Maybe, the way things seemed to go in this crazy place, they might be. It wouldn't surprise me. Nothing would. Not anymore.

Chapter 26

The car was about five miles long, the size of three normal cars strung together. It was black. A liveried chauffeur, in dove gray to match the upholstery, was the only person visible; everyone else was hidden behind tinted windows. It was vulgar, ostentatious, and utterly out of place on the Côte d'Azur, where the fashion in chauffeured cars was the Rolls-Royce.

It was pure Hollywood. You could walk stark naked down the Promenade des Anglais and not attract as many surprised glances as you would driving by, unseen, in this limousine. I was almost embarrassed to get in.

But there wasn't any choice, so I bit the bullet and climbed inside, grateful that no one I knew would be watching.

Victoria Savage had now added glasses to her costume. Like the car itself, they were black, and they covered most of her face. I wondered how she would see, now that it was dark. I needn't have worried; she could see, all right. She peered out the window at the crowds along the route, all of whom, in turn, were peering at us and trying to fathom who could be the passenger in this monstrous apparition.

"They know I'm here," she said, quite unaware that no one could see her. She touched carefully at her hair to assure herself that its perfection had been undamaged by her few steps from front door to limousine. She consulted all of us to make certain that the delicious mouth and flawless skin were unchanged by the change of scene.

Crowds had already gathered along the Promenade des Anglais, and most of the blue grandstands were filled. Flags waved everywhere. The streetlights were not yet on but would be soon; it was that magic hour on the Riviera when the stars are making their first appearance in a night-darkening sky.

Julie Savage knew how to get things done when she needed to. The limousine stopped at a barricade. The chauffeur stepped out. An envelope changed hands. And we were on our way again down the now-forbidden section of the promenade that was blocked off to all other traffic for the night. Several people clapped as we drove slowly by, thinking we must be part of the parade.

We passed the reviewing stand, still empty, in front of the Negresco. I knew it had to be the place reserved for celebrities and the mayor because it had the most flags. Victoria Savage didn't notice; she was seated on the other side of the back seat.

We continued about a block and finally came to a stop on the sea side. The "secretary" leaped out of the car and quickly cordoned off three ascending tiers of three seats each with a thick gold cord.

Only then did we descend from the car. People were just beginning to fill this section of the grandstand, and they stared at us curiously but politely. The chauffeur helped his mistress into the middle seat of the middle tier and then drove off.

"He'll be back as soon as he parks the car. You and I will sit on either side of her," Julie told me. "The two men will sit behind. The other seats will remain empty."

"I always insist on empty seats," Victoria said. "I do not like my fans too near me. I do not wish to be touched."

"It wouldn't do at all," her daughter agreed.

"And always ringside seats – second row center," her mother confided with satisfaction.

The chauffeur returned and took his appointed place behind us. The rest of the seats filled up. Hawkers began to circulate in the crowd, selling bags of confetti and candy. A festive mood now overtook those around us; they began to talk with one another, perfect stranger to perfect stranger. On all sides people whispered, asking the identity of the woman in the silver dress and dark glasses. They didn't know *who* she was; but they knew she was somebody, and that was all that mattered.

Suddenly hundreds of lights blazed on. There was a blast of music. The spectacle had begun.

The first float appeared, drowning in near-naked beauties and hundreds of live flowers. The crowd began to throw confetti. The man on my right was an American tourist who'd obviously read all about tonight's gala and had to tell me everything he'd learned.

"It's called 'Rendezvous at the Acropolis,' and it's a salute to the new center of arts and tourism here. There will be a lot of foreign groups participating: Italian flag lancers, musicians from all over Europe, dancers with colored banners, the Sixth Fleet Band, and *hundreds* of beautiful girls on the floats representing India, Austria, China, Japan, Turkey, Africa, Sweden, Italy, Canada, and the good old U.S. of A. Will you have a bonbon?" He was very excited.

I already had one. Julie had bought them from the first peddler to come our way. "Victoria adores candies," she'd whispered to me, "but Isabella forbids them at home."

The Canadian float passed, bearing a girl

with long, bare legs and a white fox jacket.

My tourist friend whistled and clapped. So did everyone else.

"Who's that next to you?" he whispered when Canada had passed.

"Movie star. Incognito." I might as well continue to play the game.

"Wow!" A marching band went by, producing deafening sounds. "Wow!"

Les Indes passed before us, drooping with exotic blossoms and a bronzed brunette clad mostly in glittering fake jewels. More cheering and confetti.

The word had now traveled through our section that we were harboring a film star incognito, and the tempo quickened. More and more confetti rained. We all were covered with multicolored dots, like figures in a pointillist painting.

Victoria Savage's silver dress gleamed in the night, so that she sat in the grandstand and sparkled like the very star she had been. The people in the parade saw the people in the stands pointing her out to one another, and before long they, too, were bowing and blowing kisses her way and throwing flowers. Like everyone else, they didn't know who she was, but they realized she had to be someone.

"They will go around and around until all the flowers have been thrown to the audience and are gone," the tourist confided in a voice hoarse from cheering.

The whole audience was shouting wildly and pelting the floats with confetti. The girls on the floats were returning the fire with flowers. The street was covered with blossoms and bits of paper. The parade moved faster and faster, now whizzing past us at astonishing speeds. The floats were nearly denuded.

Victoria Savage was infected by the spirit of the occasion without understanding what it was all about. In the beginning she had criticized the costumes and complained about the music. But as soon as the riders on the floats began to acknowledge her presence, her mood changed, and she smiled and laughed.

"Costume pictures," I heard her cry at one point, "how I loathe them. I'm always cast as some sort of dancing gypsy girl. . . . God, how I wish I'd never learned to dance!"

And another time: *"Dante and Beatrice* . . . what a love story, what an opportunity for me to show I can *act*. It was worth breaking my studio contract, I suppose. Wasn't it?"

As she said this, her mood began to alter. Her smile vanished, and her mouth fell into an angry line.

Julie tried to keep the evening glued together. *"Dante and Beatrice* was *made* for an actress with your talents. The theme was too classic for

Hollywood, even though it was a costume picture. You could only have made the film here, Victoria."

"You're right. Hollywood thought it was too literary."

"Though it was a great love story."

"No dancing. No seminude scenes. A real chance to show that I'm an artist."

"Thanks to Bordolini."

"Bordolini?" She was hesitant, frowning again.

The parade was over, the battle done. The male nurse was leading Victoria Savage down from the grandstand. The chauffeur had already gone to get the car.

There were people all over the street, gathering up the bruised and fallen blossoms.

My friend the tourist had garnered a huge bouquet. He returned with it and presented it to Victoria Savage before the male nurse could interfere.

"To you, madame . . . the most exquisite flower of the night."

Victoria Savage accepted the great bouquet graciously and turned her back on the Promenade des Anglais to face the people in the stands behind her. She looked as magnificent as a prima donna who has just brought the house to its feet with an incomparable performance.

Everyone cheered. More confetti and flowers rained down.

"Thank you all." She bowed to them and began to throw kisses.

"Bravo," they cried. "Bravo."

The limousine slid up behind her – silent and black and five miles long.

It was the perfect finishing touch. The "bravos" swelled.

"Time to go," Julie said, taking her gently by the arm.

She didn't resist. Like the true star she was, she knew the performance was over. She stepped into the limousine, and we all followed.

"My fans are wonderful," she said, sinking back into the gray velour contentedly. "The evening was a wonderful tribute to me."

Then she hesitated. "But Bordolini . . ."

She seemed to be trying to remember something.

The people all were leaving the stands at once. We were caught up in the throng, barely able to move. We were, in fact, brought to a dead halt in front of the Negresco. Everyone was gathered there in a solid, gawking, immovable mass – because the mayor, surrounded by regiments of photographers and reporters, was in the reviewing stand. Jules Ribot was granting interviews. About his absence, no doubt.

About Nice. About the *bataille*. About his political ambitions. About everything and anything. The next day the papers would report that he'd just returned from a cure, as he had been suffering from exhaustion.

He looked magnificent. The Pepsodent smile was firmly in place. And there were the usual gorgeous girls crawling all over him.

A sort of glow, the kind of aura Savage had, the aura only a real star can generate, emanated from Ribot. And I realized then what it was about the mayor: He had star quality.

God help his poor political opponents.

He began to wave to the crowd. Flashbulbs popped. The populace shouted, *"Vive* Ribot!"

I noticed Longhi and his chauffeur in the crowd. I was surprised. Julie had said the group never bothered to go; they'd all seen the parade a million times. Then I remembered that Longhi and his chauffeur were comparative newcomers.

The people were surging forward, trying to shake the mayor's hand.

No one else in the limousine noticed; they all were too engrossed in the spectacle outside. I wouldn't have noticed myself except that, as an artist I am always alerted the blink of an eyelid before anyone else.

It was only the slightest thing. She barely moved as her hand glided into her silver bag and glided out again.

There was a gleam of metal. I suppose there was also a noise, but we couldn't hear it because Ribot had just saluted the crowd and it was cheering him back.

What I did hear, what we all heard within the confines of the car, were Victoria Savage's screams.

"Bastard," she was crying, "you bastard. Look what you've done. . . . I'll kill you!"

Chapter 27

Julie Savage was wan. Even her red-gold hair had lost its luster, as if the emotions that drained the rest of us had also drained its color. "How did you do it?"

"Luck," I told her. "Just dumb luck."

She shook her head. "You have supersensitivity. Or else God was guiding you."

I was willing to let God take the credit. He doubtless deserved it. "As long as it turned out all right."

We were back at Les Fées, having sped off — if you can do that in such a big auto — as soon as we realized that no one had been hit and that no one, in fact, was even aware a shot had been fired.

The male "secretary" had wrestled the gun from Savage and given her a sedative a half second after I struck her arm and the single shot went flying into the air. He, too, had quick reflexes, and I was glad. I'm not sure I could have restrained her alone; she was surprisingly strong. I don't remember all the things she was screaming. We were too busy in the back seat to pay much attention to details like that, and once the sedative had begun to take effect, we were too busy getting her home and into the house and into bed. Isabella was in there with her, cooing over her the way one would over a baby. She had been very angry when we brought Savage home.

"I warned you, Miss Julie, I told you it was wrong. She's not strong enough for so much excitement."

And Julie had apologized humbly, like a chastened child.

The two of us were sprawled in cashmere-covered overstuffed chairs in the salon, worn out and shaken.

"I thought it would be nice. The new medication was so promising. But imagine . . ."

I didn't want to imagine. "Don't even think about it."

"But imagine if she'd killed somebody. Wounded someone even. Do you realize what that would mean? They'd put her in a hospital, and this time I would never get her out. Never. And she'd die there. She'd never survive."

"But it didn't happen. Where did she get the gun anyway?"

"I keep one. We all do, on the Riviera. There's a lot of crime, lots of robberies. Not as much here — that's why we're so grateful to

Ribot. But you never know."

"A gun, Julie? Is that such a good idea?"

"I'm a crack shot. We all are in France. *La chasse* — the hunt — is a favorite French pastime, so we're all familiar with weapons. We get invited all over during the season. We know how to shoot any kind of weapon. And it's easier than fooling with burglar alarms — all that equipment."

"But with your mother?"

She shook her head, puzzled. "I thought it was safely locked up. I haven't looked at it in ages, of course — no need to. Could I have been careless? Or could she be so sly, watching to see where I keep the key?" The thought obviously frightened her. She rose and crossed to the marble-topped table near the front door. She reached inside a vase and produced a small key, then unlocked a drawer and put the gun inside. "I'll find a new hiding place tomorrow. I still can't believe it."

I didn't blame her. After a wonderful evening that Victoria Savage had clearly enjoyed, what could have inspired the actress to such fury that she had attempted murder? And how was it possible that someone in her mental state could have planned far enough ahead to steal the handgun and take it with her?

And whom in the crowd had she tried to kill? Who was the intended victim? Who was the

219

"bastard"? There had probably been a lot of them in her life, but which of them had been worth killing? Surely not Ribot?

Or – it was an unhappy thought but no worse than those that had come before – was it just another new and terrifying manifestation of her madness?

Julie must have been thinking the same thing.

"Please don't tell anyone about this, Persis. I wouldn't want it known. It's never happened before. She's never been really violent. So please . . . I promise you I will consult with the doctor first thing tomorrow. For tonight, she is sleeping. I'm terribly, terribly sorry about all this. I had planned it to be a treat for her, a rare and wonderful outing."

She was more than dejected; she was in despair.

"There was no harm done, 'God's in his Heaven – /All's right with the world,' as Robert Browning would say."

"I know. He was inspired by living in Asolo, Italy. We lived there, too, for a while when I was little. Bordolini had a house. He left it to Mother. She went there to hide when it all went wrong. It may have been a happy place for Browning, but it wasn't for us."

She went to the curtain Isabella had pulled aside when Savage entered the room. Julie listened; there was no sound from upstairs. Savage was asleep.

Deep lavender shadows had appeared beneath Julie's eyes. It had been a terrible evening.

"You know, of course, how Mother ran away with Bordolini. He had just made a trio of great postwar films on the Riviera. . . . She married him in a civil ceremony in Nice — quite illegal, I suppose. She hadn't had time to divorce her American husband."

I knew that. Steps one and two of the burgeoning scandal.

"The Vatican excommunicated them both, as they both were Catholic and both married to other people."

Step three and the beginning of the end.

"There was a great outcry against them all through the world, and the money people withdrew their support for the film, even though it was half finished."

You could scarcely blame them. Citizens' groups everywhere, outraged and indignant, had promised to boycott the picture if it was ever released, and the moneymen had listened and prudently retreated before pouring any more into the project. Savage and Bordolini were left high and dry with a half-completed film and no funds.

"Bordolini was madly in love with my

mother, you understand, and he was determined to complete the film for her sake. So determined that he was willing to take money from any source at whatever cost."

"The Mafia," I said. "A group that had been collaborating with the Nazis in both Italy and the south of France, trading the names of freedom fighters for a guarantee of immunity to continue their own operations."

That, of course, was the *coup de grâce*. Victoria had become *persona non grata* in the film world. Sergio Bordolini was finished, even accused in the press of having been a party to Mafia activities after his return from Ethiopia in 1935 and his medical discharge from the Italian Army.

Both saw their careers disappear in a flurry of headlines and printer's ink.

Victoria then had her breakdown and began a sad odyssey from one private clinic to another, all over the Continent. There was never any question of bringing her back to America; the husband she'd run out on made certain of that by keeping the public stirred up with his ongoing hate campaign. The fact that Victoria Savage was pregnant and obviously not by her legal husband made it easier.

Bordolini, penniless, his reputation in shreds, and in debt to the Mafia, drove off the Grande Corniche and died in a flaming wreck.

Was there a connection between all that ancient history and what had happened to-night?

"Could she have seen someone tonight who had to do with all that?"

Julie shook her head wearily. "Who knows? She's ill. It could be anything. A face in the crowd that reminded her of someone . . . a shadow that brought back the past . . . something in her imagination having nothing to do with anything, making no sense at all. I'm afraid nothing has made a great deal of sense in her life for a very long time."

An act of madness — perhaps. But perhaps also an act of enormous cunning.

For she had managed to find the gun. To conceal it. To wait for a certain moment. To fire when the crowd noises would cover the sound of her shot.

She could count on the loyalty of those around her to protect her with their silence and on her history of illness to protect her even further if she were unlucky enough to be caught.

Not so mad, after all? I wondered.

"She doesn't even know I'm her daughter," Julie was saying, sadly. "She's living in 1953, and at that time she couldn't possibly have had a daughter my age. So as far as she is concerned, I'm her 'companion.' "

Had Ribot been the target, or was I letting the attempt on his life color all my thinking?

Julie was still talking; it was probably a catharsis. "Luckily for us, Mother's American business manager had invested her film earnings in California property, and eventually the money rolled in — more than we could ever need."

On the way back up Mount Boron we had been passed by a car I recognized: Nicole's gray Bentley. Everyone in our car had been too occupied with Victoria Savage to notice. The Bentley was going very fast, so I never saw who was inside.

And what about Longhi and his chauffeur? Julie was wrong when she said the group never went to the Batailles de Fleurs; tonight at least two members had been present.

And if two had been there, they all could have been there.

After all, they never did things alone.

Chapter 28

Now that he was officially back, the mayor wasted no time. The official portrait sittings began at once at his official residence in Cimiez, a big baroque heap of stone surrounded by a fortress of gates and walls.

"You'll have to forgive me – I have to continue work while you paint," he told me regretfully. "I'm so far behind now that I may never catch up. I'm paying the price of my 'cure.'"

And he slaved like a madman during every session. I was at a point where I would have liked to have him pose quietly – it would have saved time – but there was nothing to be done. I was used to it; important people never sit still.

Often the sessions lasted until two o'clock at which time the mayor flew apologetically off in one direction (presumably the Hôtel de Ville) and I in another. Sometimes I stayed on. All my materials remained there, locked up every night.

The official residence — what I saw of it in my comings and goings, which wasn't much (I was whisked down a corridor of closed doors to the mayor's office and back again without ever seeing the insides of rooms) — had an aura of unrestrained luxury. Rows of chandeliers lighted my way. Walls were massed solidly with paintings, some of which I vaguely recognized: Vertes, Brayer, Malta, Chapelain-Midy, Labisse. Carpets were so thick Napoleon's whole Army of Italy could have marched through without a sound being heard.

Even the telephones on the mayor's ornate desk were gold-colored and lavishly embellished. Surprisingly, they also worked. In fact, they never stopped ringing.

The truth of the matter was, the whole place was a bit ornate for my taste. I supposed, however, that the mayor knew exactly what he was doing; "ornate" was probably the look his electorate expected of its chief. It certainly would be good practice for the Élysée Palace.

The mayor's aides were everywhere, and so were his expanded *gardes du corps*. Having so many of the latter in evidence gave me an uneasy feeling that war might break out at any minute. On the other hand, with all this firepower around, Tendron's notion that the mayor and I might be in danger seemed laughable.

The mayor himself was quite relaxed. He

even appeared to be enjoying himself – and me. The compliments flowed. The glances were warm. The unacknowledged sparks between us flew. Without question I was territory he was planning to conquer. And the plan was all right with me.

Still, the first thing he said at the beginning of every session was always, "Well . . . have you found out yet which one of them it is?" He smiled as he said it, but I knew he was as serious as ever.

"Have you?" was my habitual response.

"Not yet. But we're close."

"I personally think you've got it all wrong. *They* are the ones who are being killed, you know. We've lost two of them so far." I still couldn't admit that his suspicions might be justified.

He was impatient with that. "Carelessness, in both instances. I have no patience with carelessness."

"What about Victoria Savage?" It was a fishing expedition, nothing more.

He laughed loudly. "What about her? Nobody's heard of her in years. Why would she want to kill me, anyway?"

"I don't know. But everyone *says* she's crazy. . . ."

He laughed again. I couldn't understand how he could be so casual. "No, no. You'll have to do better than that. Anyway, whoever it is won't get a second chance. I'll not be caught again. Immobility makes a target. If I'm a target, I'll be a fast-moving one. No one knows my schedule except me. Every place I go is thoroughly swept in advance. Everyone is checked and cross-checked — even my guards . . . no one is exempt. Look out the window."

I did. I saw silhouettes in the garden.

"Champion marksmen. Just to give you an idea. I'm always under full surveillance; we both are."

If he said it to impress me, he'd succeeded.

Then he changed the subject. "Are you going to Paris for the big bash?"

"I'm not invited. Are you going?"

"I haven't decided. Remember, the opposition is hosting this affair."

"I could call Gregor Olitsky and ask him to arrange a fanfare for you. Gregor can arrange anything."

"No, thanks. I'll decide tomorrow. I don't let anyone know my plans these days. Not even you. Not even me."

He stood up and stretched. "Nearly done, aren't you? Why not relax a little? It's time to call it a day. Feel like a swim?"

The portrait was almost finished. "No, thanks. I think I'll stay on and work a little."

"Suit yourself. But remember, life is short.

I've declared myself a holiday for the rest of today. I do it now and then; it's the only way. You ought to try it. You'll stay beautiful longer. Perhaps another time." And he left the room, his step full of a spring and an energy I hadn't seen before.

I turned back to my easel and soon lost all sense of time. I was so close to the end. It was an exciting moment, the best.

Finally I felt the fatigue. It started in my shoulders, crept down my arms, settled into my back, and exploded into a world-class headache.

I looked at my watch and was surprised to see that it was nearly five.

"Albert!" He was at my side immediately. "I've finished for the day."

"Very good, madame."

I packed up my materials and handed them to the major-domo, who disappeared in the direction of wherever they were kept. I then set off, taking my time along the corridor, walking slowly, pausing to wonder what was behind the closed doors and wishing I had the nerve to fling them open and peer inside.

One door wasn't completely closed. I suppose Albert must have come through it when I summoned him.

I saw a room with pink gauze curtains fluttering at open windows. I saw a birdcage shaped like a rajah's palace and birds chorusing inside.

I saw a Chagall.

It had the required everything: rooftops; lovers; a bouquet; the symbolic goat. It exactly matched the one in Nicole's bedroom.

But this Chagall was real.

I also saw the mayor. I saw him through the open windows. He was lounging beside a swimming pool, partially covered by a towel.

There was a magnificent girl on either side — naked. There were two young men next to him. Also naked. Very Côte d'Azur.

I was, to put it mildly, astonished. Clearly, when the mayor declared himself a holiday, he made the most of it.

What, I wondered, would have happened if I had accepted his invitation?

Chapter 29

The minute I got home I poured myself a great big drink — cognac, because it was the first thing on which I laid my hand. I have no talent for drinking; the least little thing goes straight to my head.

But this time — wouldn't you know? — nothing happened. So I poured a second drink — an even bigger one — and took it out to my front balcony and drank it down, staring thoughtfully into the purple hills where Napoleon had once marched, and even earlier, the Romans. The road from Genoa was actually called the Via Julia, and there had been Roman baths right in the garden of what became the count of Savoy's villa, now the Matisse Museum. Nearby, Roman gladiators had displayed their courage in the arena at Cimiez, where only two arches of the entry still stand.

Brave men had trodden this land. Brave men had died here.

And what of men today? A mayor had been shot. A man strangled. Another blown up.

Who would be the next to die?

The questions rattling around in my head made me very tired. The cognac didn't help either. It finally hit me like the Paris-Lyons express, and I fell into a deep, cognac-drugged sleep.

When I awoke, it was night. Across the way I saw the glow of a cigarette on my neighbor's balcony. It was nearly eleven, and it was comforting to know that he, too, was alone in the night.

Sleep was out of the question. I was slept out and wide-awake. I could hear the sound of rock music drifting up from somewhere down in the city, singers shouting their indecipherable lyrics into the amplifiers, and the cries of the concert audience cheering them on.

My world-class headache had returned, bigger than ever.

I would never get to sleep again; I knew it for a certainty.

I thought of the books my night visitor had displaced. I had shoved them back into the bookcase willy-nilly, but they didn't seem to fit. Perhaps this would be the moment to neaten up.

In my rush earlier I'd scarcely glanced at them. Now I knelt on the bare parquet floor of the library and piled them up again, intent on getting them back into their proper places. For the first time I looked at their titles.

The rest of the library was what one would expect. Gide. Proust. Balzac. An entire shelf of French *romans policiers*. Another of love stories.

But the books I'd found on the floor were different. They were all about art, and they were clearly well used, paint-spattered and worn.

The first was *Masterpieces of Art Through the Ages*.

The second was *An Artist's Handbook — Materials and Techniques*. It covered the use of oils, tempera, mural painting, pigments, grounds, watercolor, sculpture.

The third was *Identifiable Techniques of the Masters*.

The fourth was *Secrets of Fakes and Forgeries*.

The rest were more of the same, handbooks on technique mixed with small illustrated volumes on individual artists and schools of art.

I remembered the smell of paint that had pervaded the villa when I moved in. Suppose somebody hadn't painted the villa but had been painting *in it?* What was this collection of books but a forger's guide to successful deception and fraud?

Who had been living here before me? Robin Wilson. And where was Robin Wilson now? Dead.

I tried to put the books back in place. It was

no use; they wouldn't fit. No matter how I arranged them, there were always some left over. I tried every combination I could imagine. No good. Nothing worked. They must have been stacked up somewhere before without my noticing them, although it didn't seem right. Everything else was so perfectly in place, with so perfectly a place for everything.

I gave up, finally, and left the extras piled on the telephone table. My head was killing me, hammer blows of pain making my entire body shudder. The smell of paint made breathing nearly impossible. The smell was strongest in my imagination, and I knew it; but it didn't help.

What I needed was a walk. Even a small one might clear my head, make sleep possible again. Once or twice up and down the street in front of my house. It was well lighted. I would be able to breathe again. My head would feel better. I couldn't stand the villa another minute. It smelled of more than paint; it smelled of death and deception.

I carefully set my burglar alarm, then stepped out onto the sidewalk and marched briskly down the hill and around the corner that marked the far end of my property. Then I turned right so that I was now walking up the hill on the strip that divided my villa from the apartment across the street. Except for the streetlights, Mount Boron was in darkness.

I walked back and forth between my corner and the far limits of the apartment house, clearly defined in the light. Back and forth — once, twice, three times.

On the fourth trip I was suddenly not alone. I didn't hear him come; I didn't see him — he was just there.

"Madame, is it wise to be out here alone? May I accompany you?"

He was about a head taller than I would have expected, and even in the semidark I could see deep lines carved as if by a sculptor's incisive tool in a hard, lean face.

I must have made some exclamation, although I don't remember, because he tried to reassure me. "Let me present myself: Sir Geoffrey Crook, formerly head of Britain's Special Air Service Regiment, now special consultant on the formation and training of antiterrorist forces worldwide. I saw you from my balcony."

I hoped that the darkness hid my face. I must have looked like the complete fool: slackened jaw; bugging eyes; gasping breath — the works.

"You're my neighbor," I managed, finally. And not at all the kind of neighbor I had expected. "Special Air Service?"

It rang reassuring bells.

"We were the boys that broke the siege at the Iranian Embassy in 1980. What are you doing out here at this hour?"

"Headache – needed air."

"Very well, then, if it's a walk you want, let's walk. And talk."

"I was hoping," I told him (I had just that moment decided) "that we would."

No one can ever have too many friends, and he sounded like a good one to have.

We made several turns in silence. Finally we began to talk.

"Special Air Service," I began. "Isn't that called the SAS today?"

"Good girl. How did you know?" He pulled out a pipe from somewhere, and we paused while he did things to it. I didn't know anyone still smoked pipes, but it suited him.

"My father knew David Sterling, who started it in 1941 .... They met at that club, Whites." I was testing.

He knew it. "I was there at the beginning, when it was still called L Detachment. We trained at Kabrit, a hundred miles from Cairo. I was a green kid, recruited from the Scots Guards, which already had a battalion in the desert." The information was flowing to reassure me. "We were created to carry out strategic tasks: raids behind German lines, attacks on enemy headquarters, and so on, usually operating from secret bases inside hostile territory. Saw our first action in North Africa, working with the Long-Range Desert Group. Then on to western Europe. Finally, in the sixties, we evolved into an arm of the security services." His tone was frankly amused. "You're probing, and rightly so. A stranger in the night . . ."

"What happened to Sterling?" Testing again.

"Taken prisoner. Succeeded brilliantly by his brother, Bill. Satisfied?"

"Satisfied."

He performed more work on his pipe. "My last official duties before retirement were as head of the Pagoda Group of today's elite SAS corps working out of COBRA. COBRA was formed originally as an antiterrorist nerve center after two London sieges and repeated IRA bombings in mainland Britain. People forget that terrorism isn't new to us British. Today I'm called upon by many European cities and private industries to set up nerve centers in case of attack."

I wasn't surprised by any of it. The entire world seemed to me to be hostage to terrorism, which was much more real to my generation than, say, the Mafia with its men in black mustaches and funny accents.

"And you're here in Nice to —"

"Set up and supervise an international conference on terrorism. The countries of the world have finally waked up. When the offer to head this conference came in I had just come off another tough job, so I wasn't too eager. I didn't fancy being cooped up in a hot little downtown apartment. So they found me this place. View. Balcony. Place to grow things — plants are my hobby. Could I resist?"

"I saw you talking to a man named Clough-White," I said. "You know him?"

"Our paths have crossed. We've made use of his special gifts. In fact, I believe they used his connections to find me this place."

"Why did you meet on the promenade if he knew where you lived?"

Sir Geoffrey sounded distressed. "Silly old goat. He dates back to World War Two, the cold war, and bugged embassies — papers in pumpkins and all that nonsense. Doesn't realize that electronics make it all passé. Insists on meetings on street corners. Code words. Never was the real thing himself — just the odd job now and then. Remarkable memory, however. When all else failed, there was always Clough-White. Infallible."

So Clough-White wasn't a complete ninny after all.

"Silly fellow could have called me on the phone. Could have seen me at my office on the Avenue Foch or even at the airport, where we're working. No need for histrionics. But no. Secret meeting on street corner — nothing else would do. And you have to respect him —

never wrong to date."

"Did you know a man was watching you?"

Sir Geoffrey froze. "Oh?"

"The chauffeur of a geologist in our group."

"Geologist? Interesting profession. Yes, indeed." But that's all he said, and it was obvious that it was all he was going to say on the subject.

So I returned to Clough-White. "He's one of the people I work for. Why did he want to see you?"

"I know . . . The portrait. Well, it's very simple. Clough-White of the infallible memory recognized someone. Then the famous memory failed him. It took him a long time; but he pulled it out of his computer finally, and he thought I ought to know, as the information fell roughly within my jurisdiction."

I stopped walking and turned to face him. I wanted to be sure I could see him during this exchange because it was important. "Why you?"

"He knew my team and I were down here to set things up in advance of the demonstrations that would be part of the program I'd arranged. The Med region was picked for the conference because it is the scene of so much terrorist activity, as you probably are aware."

I was. And I wished Sir Geoffrey would move along faster. But he was a methodical man, with his own deliberate timetable for revealing himself. "So Clough-White recognized some-body and finally remembered who it was. Whom did he recognize that was so important he had to inform you and not the police?"

"That's one of the reasons I came down to speak to you tonight."

"What could it have to do with me?"

"He finally remembered a name."

"And?"

"The name is Maria Ponti. He'd spotted her in Nice and been puzzled for days. Who was she? Finally it came to him. He'd seen her once in Rome and she went into that famous com-puter of his. She had been a mistress of Lauro Pazzoli, leader of the gang that abducted and later murdered the Italian prime minister Aldo Moro. The Italian government is still trying to track him down. Our information is that he's lounging on the beaches of Nicaragua, which is the current surf and sand club of international terrorists."

A voice in the night. "Maria, *move on.*"

We were walking again, I not too steadily.

"All these terrorist groups," he continued, voice low, "support one another and trade information and experts: the French Direct Action gang, West Germany's Red Army Fac-tion, Belgium's Fighting Communist Cells, the lot. This girl — we're not even sure if Maria Ponti is her real name — is supposed to have

240

deserted Pazzoli in favor of one of his lieutenants, a bomb expert – identity unknown."

"Maria . . . are you crazy, standing here?" I heard the voice again.

"Clough-White, as I said, saw her once in Italy, just once, but she went into his computer. Then one day he saw her sitting at an outdoor cafe in the harbor. Le Chat Noir, he says . . . he even remembers the name of the café."

What had they said the day he went to Monte Carlo with Franck? "Clough-White's been off his feed for several days; his computer has broken down." Something like that.

"Puzzled over it for days," Crook was saying. "Finally got it straight."

"Why didn't he inform the Nice authorities?"

"Why? She wasn't doing anything. And anyway, he didn't trust them. 'Soft on terrorists,' he said. Furthermore, the mayor was out of town. 'Only go to the top,' he said. So he came to me. Obvious choice: I'm the authority on terrorism. Not to mention British." He snorted in a satisfied sort of way.

"And you?"

"Pleased as punch, naturally. Right up my alley. Obvious, isn't it? Chance to track down Pazzoli, if I play my cards right. Girl deserted him for one of his lieutenants. No red-blooded Italian accepts a thing like that. He'll surely send someone to avenge him, and that might be our chance for a big coup."

The man who had spoken to me — the lieutenant she'd run off with?

"What is she doing here?"

"Probably looking for sanctuary. Trying to arrange a deal in exchange. That's how it works."

"Why did Clough-White have so much trouble remembering, if he's such a genius?"

"Because she'd changed. Blonde now. And because of you."

I stopped again. I thought my throbbing head would fly off my shoulders and go rolling down the street like the ubiquitous French soccer ball. I almost wished it would; it was too full of things I couldn't manage to sort out. "Because of me? What do you mean by that?"

"She reminded him of you. Threw him totally off. Couldn't figure out the connection. Sister? Family? American? Threw him off the Italian track completely."

All that quizzing he'd done the day of the mad tea party. So that was it: he'd been trying to find a connection between me and an Italian girl I'd never met who reminded him of me.

"Why didn't Clough-White just ask me about her, then?"

"Thought you might be involved. Thought you might be mixed up in some plot to assassinate the mayor, he said. Asked me to check you out — didn't have the authority himself. So I did. You checked out perfectly, of course. Still, there's that other business . . . another reason I felt I had to speak to you."

What other business could there possibly be? Wasn't it complicated enough?

"Didn't take it seriously at first. Pretty girl like you — only natural. Not necessarily any harm in it. Or so I thought at first."

He paused. I guess in his profession they're not used to talking.

He drew a deep breath, like a man about to start a footrace — or jump overboard. "After Clough-White had told me about the girl, I realized it might not be so innocent. Glasses. Spot them every now and then from my terrace. Watching your house. Can't really pinpoint them — too many trees. Flash of them. Oh, yes."

After all that had come before, I wasn't even surprised. Perfectly normal. Glasses. Of course. Why not? Me and my shadow.

He paused to tap his pipe against a tree. A spark dropped onto his shirt, and he brushed at it vaguely. "I'd be careful, my dear. No wandering about alone at night. Gates and doors locked. Simple precautions."

Then it was over. . . . He saw me to my gate, waited while I turned off the alarm, waited while I unlocked my door. Waited while I turned the alarm on again.

"Remember," he called softly across the garden, "I'm your neighbor. Just shout if you need me. My men and I are at your service."

I remembered them pounding along the path on Mount Boron, and I was glad. With the former head of the SAS and all his troops on my side, who needed an army?

"I will," I called back.

I meant, I will call you, not I will need an army. It just goes to show how wrong you can be.

Chapter 30

The princess was having a dinner party.

"It's an annual event," Nicole explained. "We all wish she'd give it up, it's such a bore. But noblesse oblige, I suppose. It's the very last thing we need right now when we're all frantic with preparations for Paris."

We were rolling along in her elegant Bentley. Longhi was at the wheel, and she was seated beside him. The Clough-Whites and I were in the back. All of us were dressed to the nines for the occasion, the men in black tie and the women in long gowns. Nicole looked radiant. There was a glow beneath her transparent skin that reminded me of the glow beneath the surface of the iciest diamond. She was in sapphire, actually a dress that Poiret might have designed with its deceiving straight simplicity and intricate cut. Her black hair was drawn back in a loose chignon. Two great pearls hung from her ears, anchored in fireworks of diamonds. They were her only jewels, but they were enough.

"You look wonderful," I said.

"I'm feeling very Goya tonight," she answered.

Longhi, for once, opened his mouth. "I understand it's going to be a Goya-ish night: candles, fans, and a string ensemble." He didn't sound thrilled.

Neither did the Clough-Whites. She was wearing a one-shoulder orange crepe dress that was much too young for her. She was also wearing a tattered green feather boa, survivor of God knows what outpost gala. If her expression hadn't been so severely disapproving, she could have passed for a retired tart on the town. "It is always a painful affair," she said.

Clough-White nodded; he always nodded when his wife spoke.

"We all think," Nicole whispered, delicately arched brows rising over deep-set eyes, "that her annual dinner is lit entirely by candlelight because the house hasn't been cleaned in a hundred years and she doesn't want us to notice."

The Clough-Whites groaned in unison. I think they meant to express agreement.

I, on the contrary, was looking forward to the evening. Candlelight, and everyone ordered to carry a fan . . . At least it would be different. I'd worked hard all afternoon. The portrait was to all intents and purposes finished; it would do very well if I never laid another brushstroke on it. And Ribot loved it.

"Magnificent," he'd said. "So good, in fact, that I'm giving you a present." He'd handed me an envelope. Inside was a round-trip ticket to Paris.

I was taken fully by surprise. "I can't accept —"

But he wouldn't listen to objections. "They sent me a whole collection of tickets gratis, political plums, so it's not costing me a centime. And you said your aunt has a house in Paris, so you have a place to stay. . . ."

"True . . ."

"Well, why not, then? I'm going. We'll all be on the same flight. Actually I insist. Not the least of my reasons is that you and I might finally have a minute alone together. Dinner. Dancing. And it will be a good opportunity for me to be photographed with the artist who is doing my portrait. I need every inch of space I can get. You must do it for me."

"Well . . ."

"Good. It's settled. I'll see you on the plane." A warm, lingering look.

I'd meant to tell him about Clough-White: "You can forget about him; he's law and order." But I was so surprised that I forgot. Anyway, I'd already made it clear that there was nothing to be feared from my group of sybaritic friends. Their chief sin these days was a constant barrage of questions about the mayor: How was his health . . . how was the portrait . . . how did I like him . . . had he said where he'd been . . . when would he start going out socially again . . . was he going to Paris?

"This is our last sitting," I said instead. "I doubt if we'll have a moment alone in Paris; there will be too much going on. . . ." What I meant was, if all those warm words and intimate glances mean anything, if you're really planning to add me to your conquests, you'd better make your move now. Time is running out.

I put down my brushes and looked at him. It was one of my best days; I'd made sure it was. I was wearing my most sensational dress, the one that makes me look tall and slim and rich and glamorous. My hair was perfect, for a change, my skin was just the right shade of golden tan, and my eyes were just the right shade of greenish gray.

If he was ever going to fall upon me, gasping with passion, it was now. I would never be better.

Now or never.

I held my breath.

He stood up. He walked around his desk and came toward me, his black eyes glittering. He pulled me close against his chest. He smelled nice.

What was I going to do? Until that moment I hadn't been sure. Would I draw away? Or melt in his arms? I'd thought about it every day, but never decided.

I never found out.

"Beautiful child," he said softly. And he kissed the top of my forehead.

"Too tempting," he said, stepping back.

And, "Paris," he said, like a promise.

Then he left the room.

So that was that. I packed up and left. The war hadn't been declared. Maybe it never would be. Instead of a romantic rendezvous, I was en route to dinner with the same old group. Life is seldom fair.

In the Bentley Nicole was still discussing the princess. "You may think the fans are an affectation, Persis. But just wait, you'll see."

"See what?" Guy asked. It was to be his first visit, too.

"Never mind, I won't spoil the fun."

The invitation had arrived in the mail. It was written with great care and displayed many extravagant flourishes. It was penned on yellowing parchment beneath a crest that looked like a pastiche of eagles and crowns and randy gryphons rampant. The princess obviously was not to be outdone in matters of form.

"It's the same thing every year," Nicole explained. "There will be a few tottering wrecks removed from mothballs for the occasion, and the rest will be all of us, members of the society, meeting for the millionth time."

"There are no terraces," Clough-White said dourly, as if it explained the worst.

In fact, it did, although I didn't know it then. But I'd experienced enough of the Riviera heat to be wearing the barest, coolest thing I owned. Dull but cool. I might not stop traffic, but I would survive.

When we arrived, I wasn't exactly astounded by La Belle Époque, the princess's house; eccentric architecture was commonplace in Nice, and I'd grown accustomed to it. Still, I would have to admit that the princess's house was an extreme example of the exotic styles that abounded there.

There were cupolas. Marquees. Arches. Balustrades. Columns. Buttresses. Carvings. Stones. Stucco. Cement. Slate. Wrought iron. There was almost everything imaginable in architecture and decoration, tossed together with the reckless abandon of a salade composée designed by a disordered chef. A bewildering array of doors and arches and portes-cocheres presented themselves, and I was glad I had come with the group instead of alone; I wouldn't have known at which entrance to begin.

Actually we began at the only door that was

open. The others, as well as all the windows, were firmly shut against any intrusion of outside air.

"It's a perfect example of the kind of house that used to be called a *folie*," Clough-White's wife informed us.

"Most of them have been bulldozed down — too costly to repair," Clough-White told me. "It's a shame we can't save them. We try."

"Lunacy, foolery, folly," Nicole chimed in. "They mixed what they called *le style à l'italienne* with what they considered the last gasp in modernism — Turkish and Roman and Florentine, with balconies and animal carvings and arcades and touches of *arts décoratifs*." In spite of her complaints about the coming evening, she was displaying bursts of enthusiasm, proof that her love of architectural relics was genuine.

"And the best part," Clough-White added, "will be the princess's entrance; it's almost worth the whole insufferable evening."

"Almost." His wife underscored the qualification.

It sounded like high cinema. Hardly anyone knows how to make an entrance these days. I'd already seen one this week — Victoria Savage's. Could I be lucky enough to be about to witness another?

When we pulled up before the door, Longhi, forewarned by Nicole, refused to surrender the

Bentley to the ancient relic in crusty black who made a feeble attempt at insisting on parking it. "Once," Nicole said loudly, "he drove somebody's car over the cliff, and it came to rest in Villefranche Harbor. He's nearly blind, you see."

But he wasn't deaf, and in an obvious pet he made us wait in the doorway for Longhi to return before ushering us, none too graciously, inside the villa, where we came to rest in a black-and-white marble-floored rotunda. The rest of the guests were already assembled, fanning themselves vigorously.

"We're the last. I always plan it that way," Nicole whispered.

I was glad she had; it was stifling.

As soon as we entered, another relic — this one female and also arrayed in crusty black — began to count noses. Satisfied, she signaled to the car-parking butler, and he in turn, after several false starts, succeeded in lighting a long taper with which he then carefully lit an array of candles fixed in branched stands lining both sides of a truly extraordinary hanging staircase.

"There are twenty-six steps rising to a height of twenty-five meters," Elizabeth Clough-White announced in a hushed voice. "I've counted them."

The female retainer had labored back upstairs. Somewhere a gramophone started to play a scratchy rendition of the "Polonaise."

"Chopin," Clough-White muttered. "Terrible number."

The gramophone was turned up to its highest volume. And when it was in full cry, the princess appeared.

She was encased from head to foot in threadbare gold lamé. In honor of the occasion she had donned a gold wig, from which sprouted slightly-the-worse-for-wear fake curls. A tattered gold train trailed behind her like a moth-eaten tail. Embracing the confection of fake golden curls was a rusty tiara in which a few jewels sparkled feebly.

"All fake," someone said, sotto voce. "The real ones were sold generations ago."

The retainer was marching behind, respectfully carrying the seedy train. In the light of all the candles that lined the stairs, the retainer's musty black bombazine faded into the shadows, and only the gold of the princess's wig and gown shone dimly.

It was a real entrance. I hoped the two old ladies wouldn't fall down the stairs and spoil the effect.

The princess was descending like a Ziegfeld Girl, looking neither to right nor to left. Everyone was counting the stairs, terrified that she would step straight out into space and come crashing down on top of us.

"Twenty-six, twenty-five, twenty-four . . ." I could hear the whispered countdown all around me.

"She'll make it all right," Clough-White snorted. "She's been doing it for years."

The royal geriatric miracle continued. "Ten, nine, eight, seven . . ."

Finally the atrium was achieved, and everyone broke into applause. The princess waited gracefully for it to die down. Then, "WELCOME!" she roared. And from all sides guests threw themselves upon her, kissing her hand and drowning her in compliments.

All the ladies were by now fanning themselves, as if to stop for an instant would mean certain death.

"Would you mind?" Mario Guarnieri leaned into my self-generated breeze. "Do you suppose we could run amok and break down the shutters?"

"We might have to," I gasped.

"It will," Julie told us, "be one glass of champagne and then dinner." She was obviously a veteran of these affairs.

"You're wrong," Clough-White corrected. "It's one glass of champagne and then the chapel with the Chagall window and *then* dinner."

Before I could ask about the chapel, the two aged wrecks that passed as servants reappeared and began tottering about with champagne glasses on trays.

"Remember, it's just one drink," Mario said. "Don't rush it."

The princess was sweeping everyone into a room hung in stained brown velvet and crowned with a peeling painted ceiling on which faded cherubim cavorted dispiritedly. All the furniture was gold-colored and intricately carved and looked extremely unsafe to sit in. Stale air marched leadenly back and forth across the room, urged on by the heat from hundreds of candles, most of them held by naked bronze ladies amputated at the waists and attached uncomfortably forever to the walls.

Although we had barely arrived, I was already feeling faint from the heat, and I momentarily expected some crazed guest to tear down the draperies and claw his way outside, freeing everyone from the Polish steam bath. But looking around the room, I could spot no potential heroes; everyone seemed resigned to his fate.

"Now the chapel," the princess bellowed, "to see the stained glass window and honor my beloved son."

Son? This antiquity had once actually been wed and had produced a child from the union? Such a possibility had never entered my mind. The princess young produced no mental image;

she seemed to have been born exactly as she was today – knotty veins and all.

There was no time to ask anyone if I had heard correctly. We were swept helter-skelter through a series of dingy rooms and into a small chapel lined with great bunches of artificial flowers and presided over by a gigantic gold cross. A big purple and blue stained glass window more or less lit the room, and carved in the wall on either side of the cross in wobbly letters that might well have been by the princess's own hand was the legend:

HONOR TO
PRINCE DARIUS WYDZINSKI
HEROIC POLISH DRAGOON
B. 1912 D. 1954 A.D.
MOURNED IN ETERNITY

The other guests were familiar with the drill. Each took a slender white candle from an offered box, lit it, and placed it on one of the spindles forming rows in front of the cross. The chapel came alive with flickering tongues of light.

After they had lit their candles, the guests knelt briefly before the cross, then filed toward the back of the chapel. The princess remained kneeling, flanked by her two antiquated servants.

Suddenly she cried out in an ear-shattering voice: "My hero son, you are not forgotten."

I had the impression that we were all supposed to say "Amen," but nobody did.

What I did hear was somebody saying, "The bastard."

I almost dropped my candle. But the princess was oblivious.

"My hero son!" she cried once more. The chapel walls trembled.

Then, with no more ado, she allowed herself to be helped to her feet and began marshaling her troops for the next act.

"Dinner is now being served," she shouted.

We all set forth again.

"The cook," Guarnieri said in my ear as we marched to the buffet, "is as blind as the butler. She doesn't know a ham from a tire washed up on the beach at Menton."

Mustard chimed in. "You'll find that the beef was a calf in approximately the time of Alexander the Great. Don't touch it."

I wondered what I *was* supposed to touch: The ham and the roast beef were the chief offerings on the table. At least they were identifiable. Everything else, barely discernible in the flickering candlelight, was a mystery.

I needn't have worried. As I passed along the length of the buffet table, various offerings were slammed down on my plate by the two aged domestics with no regard to choice.

"Why can't we serve ourselves and let the two old wrecks go to bed where they belong?" B. B. Benezit asked crossly.

"She says it was always this way in the days of the Polish court," Mustard told her.

"I doubt it. It's just that she's too cheap to do a dinner party right. It's a disgrace."

Having not yet dined at the Benezit-Mustard villa, I wondered if I was to expect platoons of servants when I did.

We all were milling around, trying to find our place cards at the great long dining table.

"Isn't this a bore? You're over there, Persis. I just passed your card. Have you seen mine?" Julie looked frantic; damp ringlets of hair were plastered to her forehead.

"I didn't know she had a son," I said vaguely, to no one in particular.

"Ha!" Guarnieri took my elbow. "We're over here, Persis . . . this way. As to her son — ha!"

"You said 'ha' . . . why?" I trotted after him obediently.

He was right. There we were, our names shakily inscribed on china place cards, side by side.

We sat down. We bowed to the people on our other sides. We took a sip of our wine.

"I said 'why,' Mario?"

"Because if it weren't for Ribot," he answered, "the princess would have been run out of Nice long ago."

"Whatever for, Mario? She's only a poor old woman. Why?"

"Because 'collaborator' is still a strong word in France — even today. It's as strong a word as 'murderer' — maybe stronger."

"You're saying the son was —"

"Yes. And eventually found out and executed by the survivors of the maquis. It's how they did things."

"But Ribot?"

"He and the son went to school together, were in the same resistance cell. There was a certain loyalty."

The string ensemble had taken up its instruments and begun to play something unrecognizable. It would have been better if they had been playing in the next house or the next town. They were awesomely bad.

Longhi passed, bearing a plate. "Be of good cheer," he said. "Nicole says dessert is to be a chocolate mousse — she peeked. And she recommends that we go in search of an ax."

When I turned back to Guarnieri, he was engaged in deep conversation with the lady on his left. And he stayed that way.

In due time the chocolate mousse arrived. It was as promised — terrible. Longhi saw me address myself to it, and he winked from across the table.

I fanned at the gentleman on my right to keep him from expiring. I listened to the deafening screeches of the string ensemble.

The candles flickered. Plates arrived and disappeared.

"The mousse," said the gentleman on my right, "is, er, remarkable."

"Quite so," I agreed.

Far be it from me to suggest that the mousse was less than perfect. I was, after all, a guest.

Nor would I suggest either that the Chagall stained glass window in the chapel was less than perfect. It wouldn't have been polite.

Yet it was fake.

As fake as the Chagall in Nicole's bedroom. Somehow, it didn't surprise me in the least.

Chapter 31

With the portrait finished, all that remained for me in Nice were the presentation ceremonies, scheduled to take place after everyone's return from Paris.

Exactly three weeks after my arrival in Nice I would be back in Gull Harbor.

I was still in my evening dress, still reeling from the princess's party, still stunned by the revelation that the princess had had a son, that he had been a collaborator, and that Ribot had been his friend.

Sitting on the edge of my bed, light from the bedside lamp streaming across me, I picked up my sketchbook and began to draw likenesses, cartoons almost, of everyone involved. It is my time-honored remedy for soothing body and spirit and, more important, for sorting things out in my mind. There's something about it that works for me; the visual stimulates the mental. Things fall into place. I can't explain why, but the system rarely fails.

I wanted to begin with Ribot, who was the

hub of it all, but it was no use. It was as if the whole Society for the Preservation of Old Nice had risen in protest and demanded that their likenesses be done first. There was no point in resisting; it was easier to give in. So I did them, one after the other, thumbnail sketches in quick strokes that caught the essence of each subject. Spare but telling. And I tried to add a mental line or two beneath each sketch to clarify why that particular person might have had reason to kill Jules Ribot.

Nicole first: A society beauty jilted by a man whose career she had set on the track to success. Motive number one? Further, she was minus an important painting, which I had recently seen in Ribot's official residence. Motive number two?

Anton Franck: Retired Mafia chieftain posing as a Greek banker, possibly linked in the past through business holdings to Ribot. No visible motive, inasmuch as Franck was now dead. (Investigation of cause still in progress.)

Princess Anna: Impoverished Polish nobility, parent of alleged Nazi collaborator. Allowed to remain in Nice through good offices of son's former comrade-in-arms, Ribot. Was it possible she would want to destroy Ribot because he might have proof of her son's treachery?

Mario Guarnieri: Former Grand Prix driver still using a *nom du sport*, eternally pursuing

World War Two information and supposedly writing a book, despite being considered an "intellectual illiterate." Did the mayor perhaps know his real name and was there something else involved?

Julie Savage: Devoted to a mother whose film career had washed up on the shores of the Baie des Anges. Would she shoot the mayor to protect her mother for reasons unknown?

Victoria Savage: Mother of Julie. Had tried to shoot *someone*. Could it have been Ribot — again for reasons unknown?

James Gallop Mustard and B. B. Benezit: Currently living well with no visible means of support. At first glance, neither had a motive for killing Ribot, but both had motives for killing Robin Wilson — the motive in each case being jealousy.

Robin Wilson: Bisexual self-proclaimed hard-up dancer rescued by Mustard. Evidence at L'Oasis suggests he was actually a starving artist, not a dancer at all, and that — with the inspiration and assistance of Mustard and Benezit? — he ran a neat little business painting copies of stolen masterpieces, from what was now my villa. Had he sold the Chagall to Ribot? Had Ribot become his lover? Was Ribot the source of the gold watch, etc., etc.? Was Wilson the motive for Mustard or Benezit to try to kill Ribot? Did Mustard and Benezit, in their Riviera travels, select the "marks"? Did Mustard and Wilson engineer the thefts, Wilson paint the copies and peddle the originals for them? Had Ribot found out?

The Clough-Whites: Retired civil servants — he a human computer who had recently identified Maria Ponti as the mistress of a wanted Italian terrorist. Did this tie in with Ribot? If so, how?

Guy Longhi: Alleged geologist, with an unlikely chauffeur who spied on people. I would not trouble myself about him. I had a pretty clear idea of his motives for everything. Maybe.

Twelve people, counting Victoria Savage. Twelve question marks, some bigger than others.

I sat for a long time, staring at my drawings and matching them to my unwritten lists. The answer was there. I sensed it. It was at my fingertips.

I put my sketchbook down and began to prowl the villa. Motives, answers — all there, just beyond my reach. Tantalizingly near, but just eluding me.

I went from room to room, switching on lights, switching them off again. Sir Geoffrey had said someone was watching me. Longhi? His "chauffeur?"

Someone else?

I returned to my sketchbook. It was time for

the mayor now. Finally. He came to life in a few sure strokes. After all, I knew him by heart, didn't I? This time, just to vary the routine, I sketched him as I'd seen him lounging at the pool. Dark. Lean. Laughing. Irresistible. A towel flung casually across his middle.

And there it was. Right there — on my sketchbook page. Staring me in the face. Clear, if I'd thought about it instead of being so dazzled, from the very first day.

Finally.

I put my sketchbook down and sat very still for perhaps five minutes, sorting it out. Then I went to the telephone.

The telephone at the other end rang and rang. Naturally, anyone with any sense had been asleep for hours. Outside the library windows I could see the first streaks of dawn tinting the sky over Cimiez.

Finally the ringing stopped.

"Yes?" The voice was thick with sleep.

"Ed Simms told me once, but I forgot. 'The unlikeliest cover is the best,' he said. And you picked a lulu, I must say."

"Oh?" The voice was wide-awake and clear now, all trace of sleep erased.

"What's more, the airplane we're scheduled to fly on will never get to Paris. It will blow up. So simple, really . . . I don't know why I didn't see. But I had it backwards, as usual."

"Whoa ... wait ... what are you talking about?" Sharply. No leftover sleep.

"You'd better come. We haven't much time, geologist. And bring your fellow agent, the famous 'chauffeur.' "

Silence at the other end.

"Deuxième Bureau," I said, to make it clear, "I need you."

"I'll be right there." And Longhi hung up.

Then I called Crook.

Chapter 32

Like everything else it did, the group's departure for Paris was organized to revolve around food.

"We will get an early start for the airport and breakfast there. We can have champagne; it will ease the pain of flying."

The luggage, mountains of it, would go in Nicole's car with her driver. The group itself would be transported in a fleet of taxis to avoid the ennui of having to park cars at the airport.

Ribot was sending his car for me; he had been adamant. "It's the least I can do. I'll meet you there." There was no choice but to acquiesce gracefully. It wouldn't do to rock the boat. Not with anybody. Not now.

I was beginning to get edgy by the time the Peugeot finally arrived; it was late. Not that I'd mind missing breakfast; I was too nervous to think of eating.

This early in the morning Nice — devoutly night-oriented to pleasure — was like a deserted city. The stoplights along the promenade weren't on yet; they were still set for blinkers only. The planted center divider was being watered by a sprinkling system. Men in rubber aprons were hosing down the sidewalks. A single youth in shorts was churning along the esplanade, running his heart out. Opposite the boarded-up Palais de la Méditerranée, victim of the famous wars of the casinos, a white blood bank truck and station wagon were setting up, preparing to waylay sleepy citizens on their way to work.

The Peugeot sped along. The driver did not speak except to say that Ribot was not coming. But I had expected that.

At the airport the machines dispensing parking tickets had not been turned on for the day, and inside the terminal airline personnel were lined up neatly behind their *ordinateurs;* but there were as yet no clients. The waiting rooms were empty. Ours was the first flight of the morning.

As I stepped inside, a uniformed airline official appeared from nowhere. He relieved me of my bag and escorted me to the counter. A young girl in Air-Inter's distinctive dress approached and signaled me to follow her. She opened a door behind one of the counters and whisked me through. It was done very quickly. I felt like Alice disappearing down the rabbit hole.

"Is everything all right?" I asked as I followed her along some nonpublic passage.

Her heels beat a castenet rhythm on the corridor floor. "Perfect." She paused suddenly and opened another door. We dived inside.

"You will wait here, please . . . it won't be long. We'll be back for you."

"The others?"

"All set." She opened the door and left in a rush.

I was in somebody's office. The furniture was the usual unreliable-looking French contemporary plastic. The walls were the usual poisonous greenish brown. The desk had no papers.

I settled down in one of the plastic chairs, not without misgiving.

Time passed. I studied the room's only artwork, a large poster advertising an exhibition at the château in Cagnes-sur-Mer. I studied it several times. It must be departure time. Or almost.

The announcement system sprang suddenly to life. "The departure of the Air-Inter flight to Orly West will be delayed. . . . The departure of Air-Inter flight Sixteen to Orly West will be delayed. . . ." The voice on the public-address system was as feminine, sexy, and alluring as a voice inviting a gentleman to bed.

More time passed. I was beginning to get jumpy.

Then, suddenly, the Air-Inter girl was back. "Please follow me — and hurry."

On the way down the hall I saw a clock, and noted the time: 7:15 A.M.

It was like a very short forced march. We charged down a series of corridors and out a fire door and onto an airport bus. The whole thing didn't take a minute.

Then we were speeding across the tarmac toward the end of the landing field. The windows of the bus were so dirty I could barely see out, could barely discern the shape of another bus speeding by us in the opposite direction, or the form of the aircraft we circled. On the far side the driver threw on his brakes. "You will board as quickly as possible."

An assortment of passengers, including the board, piled out of the bus and hurried across the short expanse of runway to the metal stairs. Crew members in the open doorway waved us forward impatiently. The door shut. The engines revved up. The aircraft eased forward.

The flight to Paris had begun.

The aircraft began its graceful arc out over the sea. Young children began a parade to and from the bathrooms. Hostesses passed out newspapers. The captain switched off the seat belt sign. One of the children began to wail, and three stewardesses rushed to comfort it.

Passengers on the right side of the plane, who had been savoring their last glimpse of the Côte d'Azur, suddenly gasped and began to exclaim aloud. A passing stewardess looked out the window and then, without a word, hurried forward to the curtained cockpit section.

The intercom switched on, and the captain's voice filled the plane.

"Ladies and gentlemen, this is Commandant Janson speaking. I very much regret to tell you . . . something very unfortunate . . . something terrible . . . there has been an explosion . . . The airport . . ."

He did not finish. No one really expected him to. It didn't matter; all the passengers were busy talking among themselves. There was a rush to the right side of the plane, followed by cries of shock and dismay.

I was seated next to a window. I had seen it all, from the first flash to the black smoke that was now turning to distant white plumes as it ascended into the chaste blue sky.

The captain was back on the intercom. He had his voice under control now. It had recovered the deeply male authority that is part of a commercial aircraft captain's mystique in every language.

"Ladies and gentlemen . . . Captain Janson again. We have been in touch with the tower and have more details for you. An Air-Inter plane has been blown up and destroyed on the ground at Nice International Airport. There has also been an explosion inside the terminal. I will have more information for you as it becomes available. At this moment there is no report on casualties or the identity of the perpetrators. The airport is closed; we're the last plane."

The princess, who was seated on my left, leaned across me to see out the window and pinioned my dress to my thigh with curved nails mercifully sheathed in white cotton gloves.

"Vot iss dot?" she bellowed in my unprotected ear.

" 'We expect a philosophy of life,' " I told her, "and we get nothing but a turgid melodrama.' I'm quoting."

"Quodink? I done onderstand."

A touch of insanity had infected me. "No reason to understand. I'm not sure that I do myself. I quote the critic Meier-Graefe because he put it very well, although in another context. I believe he was referring to the grotesqueries of the German secessionist artist Böcklin. That was in 1908, but it does seem apropos. Grotesqueries are grotesqueries."

The princess was irritated. She made it quite clear. "Meier-Graefe, Böcklin . . . Airport goink up in smoke and you're sayink. . . ?"

I sighed. It had indeed been a turgid melo-drama. But she was entitled to an answer. "The great artist Sir Joshua Reynolds once said in an address to his students, 'All the objects which are exhibited to our view by nature upon close examination will be found to have their blem-ishes and defects.' I believe he made this re-markably astute remark in about 1770."

She was at the end of her patience. "So?" Even with the noise of the engines as competi-tion, the single word would shatter glass.

It had been the worst of days. But I tried. "What I am saying, what I think I am saying, Princess . . . is that I will never, under any circumstances, paint another portrait."

"Oh." She was disappointed. "I thought it had somethink to do with . . . that." She waved at the window.

"Believe me, Princess," I whispered, "it does."

Chapter 33

Our arrival at Orly was surrounded by chaos.

Cameras everywhere. Reporters running along at passengers' sides, shouting. Microphones thrust into faces. Light bulbs flashing. TV cameras. Police trying to restore order. Special police trying to isolate the passengers.

Antenne One and Two trucks outside. People swarming. Horns. More shouting. Jostling. Radios blaring. Cameras grinding.

Near panic.

"What do you know about —"

"What did you see —"

Gregor trying to whisk me away, and succeeding, finally. Taxi radio screeching: "Mayor of Nice announces terrorist attack on Nice International Airport. Air-Inter plane destroyed on ground. Estimated one hundred twenty-seven passengers dead. Second bomb detonated in airport lounge. Casualties as yet undetermined. Branch of Pazzoli group credited. Tie-in to death of Aldo Moro. Mayor says two terrorists in custody. . . ." On and on.

"Turn it off, please."

Gregor wasn't listening. "God, Persis, I'm so grateful you weren't on that plane."

"Please turn it off." I couldn't stand it anymore. Not at this moment.

Gregor wasn't listening, but the driver heard; he switched off the radio, grumbling.

"Anyway," Gregor was saying, "you're here — and in one piece. I'm surprised."

"It wasn't exactly the way I'd planned it. In fact, I hadn't planned to come. Not until the last minute."

Gregor wasn't interested in how or what I'd planned; he never was. "Well, the point is that you're here. So let's get on with it. I've arranged for some interviews. The press will want you with the portrait . . . and there are these receptions. . . ."

Gregor was an incurable pragmatist. He didn't care who blew up whom or what or where so long as it didn't involve him and his affairs. The next luncheon, the next dinner, the next exhibition, the next ball, the next picture sold were what interested him.

I had expected nothing more.

He probably won't even notice when the next disclosures are announced, I thought.

And I was right. He didn't.

They came while we were at cocktails in the Baroness von Klimpt's suite at the Meurice —

she always favored the Meurice, Gregor said. It was the first in a series of receptions.

He was giving the baroness, who was very rich and very ignorant about art, the full benefit of his considerable charm. A new arrival whispered something about the news. Somebody went into another room and turned on the TV. The word spread and one by one, everyone went in to listen.

Everyone but Gregor and the baroness.

They were too absorbed in each other to be interested.

"Gregor," somebody finally said, "there's some important stuff about Nice coming in on the TV. You ought to hear it."

He didn't even turn around.

"Gregor," the person persisted, "you really ought —"

This time he answered. But not until he had taken the baroness's hand in his.

"How," he asked, "can they interrupt me when I am mining gold?"

The baroness loved it. She laughed a deep, rich laugh that sounded like coin of the realm dropping into a private safe. And she leaned forward and kissed Gregor on the forehead.

"Mr. Olitsky," she said, "you are a devil!"

It was no more than I had expected.

Chapter 34

It had been forty-one hours since Nice, and we'd seen one another constantly. Dinners. Receptions. The vernissage. The gala afterward.

But that had all been while we were surrounded by a cast of thousands. Now, finally, it was over, and we were alone.

It had begun with an animated discussion of where to meet. It was a matter of selecting another restaurant, which was only normal, because we were gathering for yet another meal.

"Taillevent," someone suggested.

"Le Grand Véfour," somebody else insisted.

"I know a quiet little fish restaurant around the corner from the Musée Rodin." I was surprised to hear myself speak. It was the first time I had ever suggested anything. And here we were. "It's time Persis got to choose," someone had said magnanimously.

Luckily the menu wasn't letting me down. On the contrary, it was excelling itself. So far they had deliriously sampled scallops in a gossamer cream sauce with truffles, poached oysters in white wine and crème fraîche, and a sea urchin roe blended with an exotic butter none of us could identify.

The crisp St.-Aubin Burgundy we were drinking also elicited groans of pleasure.

James Gallop Mustard and B. B. Benezit weren't present. "Where are they anyway?" somebody demanded, annoyed by their defection. "We haven't seen them since the plane."

"Decamped," I told them. "Ever since the police started investigating the explosion of Franck's yacht, they've been afraid the law had stumbled on to their scam."

They were all attention. "Scam . . . does that mean crooked business?"

"Exactly. I should have realized it when I stepped into L'Oasis the first time. The smell of paint was strongest in the library, because that's where Wilson painted. He wasn't a dancer at all; he was an artist. Hopeless at anything original — there are a lot of them like that — but an inspired copyist of everything from oils to stained glass. Mustard saw the possibilities at once. Benezit selected the marks; with her entrée and expertise it was easy. Mustard and Wilson abducted the art — easy also, as nobody on the Riviera bothers with security. The owners ransomed

back the copies — they didn't know the difference — and the originals were sold by the
charming Wilson to collectors looking for a
bargain. It was a lucrative operation, although I
gather most of the money went into Mustard
and Benezit's pockets and not into Robin's."

Nicole swallowed a scallop whole and began
to choke. There was a minute or two of back
thumping before she could speak again. *"My*
Chagall?"

"Afraid so — probably one of Wilson's best
works. The original hangs on Ribot's wall."

She gave a cry of pain. "He always coveted
that painting. I say *damn* Ribot."

We all fell silent while the waiter poured
more wine.

Then the princess shouted, "I say so, too.
Damn Ribot. First he seduct my son. Then he
betrayt him. My son vas innocent. His only sin
vas a veakness in *loff*."

Julie Savage looked devastated. "I say damn
him, too. He made my mother go to bed with
him to get money for her film when the other
backers withdrew. She did it for Bordolini. It
was Mafia money and a terrible scandal when it
came out. But the real tragedy was that Ribot
got her pregnant, and Bordolini knew it wasn't
his child. It couldn't have been; he was shot up
in Mussolini's Ethiopian adventure. It wasn't a
gallant war. Only fifteen hundred Italian sol-

diers were killed in that campaign, but Bordolini might as well have been. When he found out about Ribot, he drove himself over the side of Mount Boron. And Mother . . . she wanted Ribot dead, too. She tried to kill him. Imagine, Ribot . . . my father!"

Julie began to cry. The *patron* rushed over, all solicitude. "Mademoiselle . . . mademoiselle . . ."

She wiped her eyes. "It's all right. I have to live with it."

The *patron* withdrew.

It was Guarnieri's turn.

"Ribot betrayed my brother to the Nazis. I've never been able to prove it, but I'm getting closer every year, every day. Even back then he would do anything to save his neck: betray one comrade to the Nazis and another to the maquis, and neither of them guilty of anything except knowing him."

"Ange Grasso," I said. "Your brother. You were looking for —"

"Yes." Mario drew himself up. "There is no book."

Clough-White's rust-stained mustache twitched angrily. "And to think I almost told him about Maria Ponti. Imagine!"

"Why are we all alive?" his wife demanded. "Weren't we supposed to have been killed?"

"You bet. We were all supposed to die in a

plane bombing; and you can thank two men that we didn't, Longhi, who knows how to get things done. And a man named Crook, who had constructed a model of an Air-Inter plane exactly like the one we were to fly on to Paris — a model to be used for demonstrations of the latest antihijacking techniques at the International Conference on Terrorism. He had a crack team there, practicing. He had already set up a scenario for aircraft and airport bombings. All materials and personnel were at hand. It was the perfect opportunity for a dry run: to blow up the model plane and simulate the bombing of the airport."

"Longhi?"

The whole world didn't have to know who and what he was. They didn't have to know that he was Secret Service, that he was on the Côte d'Azur because a fellow agent had been killed and his body dumped at Aspretto, near the combat swimmers' base. The Deuxième Bureau suspected the trail led back to the Mafia, which the agent had been investigating, and thence to Ribot.

"As I said, Longhi has clout. Remember, he's a friend of the widow of d'Esmé, late minister of defense. He had the power to do what was necessary." They needn't know more.

The waiter arrived to take the orders for our main course, which we still hadn't selected. All insignificant conversation was shelved while the truly serious matter of food was addressed.

A prayerful quiet prevailed.

Finally the nearly impossible choices were made, the tension was relieved, the conversation allowed to resume.

"How did *you* know, Persis?"

There was a certain pique in the way they asked — a certain wounded vanity. I was the newcomer, supposed to know nothing. They were the board, supposedly omniscient. Things were decidedly askew.

"It wasn't easy. I should have guessed the night my house was broken into. Nothing was disturbed but some art books that wouldn't fit back on the shelves. I ought to have guessed why — because they hadn't been *on* the shelves in the first place. Someone broke in not to steal anything, but to add something — the books. They were meant to convince me that I was dealing with a bunch of terrible people. Forgers . . . thieves . . . maybe worse."

"Poor Robin, he would do anything for money," Nicole said dryly.

"Then there was the mayor's apparent conviction that someone among you wanted to kill him. But I was equally convinced that while a number of you might *want* to kill him, you never would."

Guarnieri wasn't so sure. "I might have."

"No, you're too kind. Anyway, the girl, Maria Ponti, was the key. She'd come here with her lover, knowing that certain Mafiosi lived here undisturbed because Ribot had ancient ties with them. She went to see the mayor, armed with the threat to bring up his old connections – surely embarrassing to him during a presidential bid – knowing nobody else would have her because of *her* involvement with the Moro killing, unable to use her terrorist connections because she had deserted Pazzoli, hoping to strike a deal for sanctuary. When you people proposed me to the mayor, he saw a resemblance and an opportunity to use that resemblance to dispose of all of you, which he believed was necessary because each of you had information that could sink his presidential ship. He asked for more photos of me, satisfied himself that Ponti was a good enough look-alike, and went into action."

I took a long sip of wine, exhausted by all that talking. They had actually stopped eating and were staring at me, bewitched.

"The plan hinged on our trip to Paris," I continued. "But first there was a matter of the two who weren't going, Wilson and Franck. Wilson was blackmailing Ribot about his sexual activities, which were scarcely presidential in nature; Franck was under investigation and might have let something slip about the old Mafia alliance. So Ribot assigned Ponti and her lover to do away with them — part of the price of sanctuary — and they did."

"Ribot, Ribot . . . always Ribot?"

"Always. His plan began when you proposed me. He pretended to be shot so as to cast doubt on you and wrap himself in a cloak of innocence; you must remember that he knew I had ties with the press through Tendron and that Tendron would be interested in everything I did. He wanted to establish the myth that *you* were the villains. To that end he had me followed, watched, trying to frighten me, and planted the evidence in L'Oasis against Wilson, Mustard, and B. B. He thought of everything. The Gainsborough Brown gala in Paris was the perfect opportunity to dispose of us all at the same time by blowing up the Air-Inter plane and everyone on it in what would appear to be part of a terrorist attack on the Nice airport."

"No!"

"The girl and her lover would plant the explosives in the plane and in the airport itself. Her job was to wait until I left the passenger lounge, then return with her duplicate of my ticket and pretend she'd forgotten to check one bag. That bag would hold a bomb. Her cohort's assignment was to plant yet another bomb in the waiting room."

I paused. They didn't say a word this time. They were too stunned.

"In any case," I resumed, "Crook's team was ready for them. They dispatched a bus full of personnel impersonating passengers to the pseudo Air-Inter plane so Ribot's agent wouldn't suspect anything. We were driven to a different plane at the far end of the runway. The real bombs were rounded up by Crook's team. Dummy bombs were exploded. Ponti and her lover were collected – they'd been under surveillance the whole time, naturally – and the mayor –"

"Ribot?"

"You know the rest."

They did. And they actually stopped eating and drinking long enough to reprise it. "Rushed to the airport to announce triumphantly that there'd been a terrorist attack and that the airport and the aircraft had been bombed. Two wanted terrorists would be in custody shortly, he said. Naturally, he was going to betray them, probably say that they had been 'shot while trying to escape.' Imagine his shock when Crook informed him that the bombing had actually been a practice exercise, in the course of which his men had apprehended two terrorists who were now ready to talk."

Everyone looked bemused, imagining the

mayor at that moment.

"There was no scar when I saw him by his swimming pool," I told them. "I didn't realize it at the time. Nor did I pay attention the very first day, when he put his hands behind his head and forgot to wince. He was careless, but so was I."

"And that's how you guessed?"

"Partly. But there was a final clue."

"Which was?"

"You said he was a ladies' man — a lover . . ."

"*Anybody's* man . . . women or men . . . it didn't matter."

"Anyway, a lover?"

"Right," they said.

"Well, that was the final clue."

"What was?" They were exasperated. "What happened?"

"Nothing. That's exactly it."

"Explain, please."

"He never made the tiniest pass at me. Not seriously. It was quite insulting."

"What?" They didn't believe me.

"The great lover. And when he had me to himself . . . quite willing . . . *nada* . . . zilch . . . *rien* . . . nothing."

I sat back then and waited for it to happen, and it did. First they smiled behind their napkins. Then they giggled. Then they roared with laughter until they almost cried. "The

286

best clue of all, the best clue!"

I thought they'd never stop. It was a most unusual display. The staff of the restaurant was aghast; the French don't carry on like that in public.

"We'll never be able to eat here again," Julie gasped finally. "Too bad — the food is excellent."

That brought them to their senses.

"There is one thing." Nicole's eyes were misty and perhaps not from laughing. "He was a help to our cause after all. Indeed, in the end he did the honorable thing."

She meant, I suppose, that when the jig was up, he took a leaf from Bordolini's book and drove himself off the side of Mount Boron to his death.

"No one," she continued thoughtfully, "will ever know the truth. As far as the world is concerned, he died in an accident that ended a brilliant political career on the threshold of further triumphs. If the two terrorists talk, who will believe them if nobody backs them up? No. We will continue with our plans. We will present the portrait of our beloved mayor to the city of Nice in a memorial service. It will be a grand occasion — one that should inspire his successor to support our cause. Agreed, board?"

"Agreed."

She raised her glass. They raised theirs. "To Ribot."

"To Ribot!"

Everybody drank.

"And afterward," Nicole went on, into the spirit of the thing now, "we will all go to Roger Vergé's at the Moulin de Mougins for dinner."

I left them discussing it, the princess roaring about meringues and the Clough-Whites gasping with anticipation. I had a plane to catch. It was time to go home.

But I left smiling. I'd thought before I came to Nice that the people would be the best part, and they hadn't let me down – not for an instant.